She'd remember Paul and wonder about him

It was almost entirely physical, Anna told herself, the attraction between them. It had to be, because she knew nothing about him and she was not in the habit of falling in love with strangers.

She felt guilty about Douglas, angry with herself. Douglas...she couldn't even remember what he looked like. She twisted his engagement ring on her finger restlessly.

"Take that damn ring off," Paul said hoarsely, pulling her close. "Stay with me."

She closed her eyes. "I don't want to stay. I want to go home." She was shaken by the violence of her heartbeats. His dark eyes gleamed with mockery.

"Are you afraid I'll try to make love to you? Or afraid that you'll let me?"

Other titles by
JANE DONNELLY
IN HARLEQUIN ROMANCES

A Savage
Sanctuary

by

JANE DONNELLY

Harlequin Books

TORONTO · LONDON · NEW YORK · AMSTERDAM
SYDNEY · HAMBURG · PARIS · STOCKHOLM

Original hardcover edition published 1979
by Mills & Boon Limited

ISBN 0-373-02293-X

Harlequin edition published in November 1979

CHAPTER ONE

THE women thronging the fabric department of Pattersons on the first day of the Autumn Sale were mostly home dressmakers, looking for bargains that would make up a dress or a suit or a skirt. Or something for the children. Or a pretty piece of brocade for a cushion.

But the girl who was going through the bins of assorted scraps was an artist. She touched the fabrics as though the textures gave her a sensual satisfaction, rubbing, stroking, her shining eyes ranging over the massed mixed colours.

She went away with a bagful of pieces and the woman on the till, who was used to seeing Anna Cameron going through the remnant tray and thought she was very talented, asked 'What's this lot going to be? A patchwork quilt?'

'Some of it,' said Anna, with a happy grin, hugging her bulging canvas bag; and as she threaded her way out through the shoppers the woman on the till told the next two in the queue:

'That's the girl who makes those gorgeous wall panels and quilts and things they sell in Bissells.'

At twenty-one Anna was doing nicely. She loved her work, really loved it. Her father had been an amateur artist and Anna had gone to art school because she had a feel for colour and line.

She had always made her own clothes, but when she made a surprise wall hanging for a friend's birthday it was so successful that she found herself inundated with orders, and then she realised that she was happier with a needle than a brush. She had been studying graphic art

5

and she began combining pictures with sewing, painting less and less, sewing more and more. She finished her course, got her degree, but now she only sketched and painted to work out a design before she began cutting and stitching and embroidering.

She had a very special design on her mind today. Such a lovely day it was, with an autumn nip making the air like wine, and sunshine making the colours so clean and bright.

She was a long-legged girl, striding along in soft leather boots the colour of horse chestnuts, wearing a full-skirted russet dress and a matching suede waistcoat. Her hair was the same autumn colour, and her eyes were very clear, amber-brown, fringed with thick lashes.

She walked fast. She had done all she came out to do, and now she was on her way home, and there was a feeling of vitality and purpose about her. That, and her striking prettiness, made people turn to watch her. Men in particular. If she had been lingering she would have been chatted up, but she wasted no time.

She was in a hurry to get back and sort out her spoils and settle down again to the design that was waiting on her drawing board. Thinking of that made her smile, lifting the corners of her wide mouth. She had just over a week to complete the embroidered picture, because next week Bissells were putting on an exhibition of her work.

It wouldn't be the first exhibition. She had been selling through them ever since she started her career as needle-woman over a year ago. This would be the second time that the small salon on the ground floor, where the work of selected artists and craftsmen was shown, had been given over to the creations of Anna Cameron.

But this time was special and she was sewing a special picture for Douglas with a sunburst theme, representing the golden joy of life she felt when she was with him. Because she was one of the family now. She would be

Anna Bissell in the spring, married to the son of the man who owned the Galleries. She had been wearing Douglas's ring for the last month and she had been in love with him for much longer than that. Perhaps for ever. She had known Douglas Bissell by sight all her life. He was five years older than she was and he had hardly noticed her until she took her sewing samples into the Galleries during her last days at art school. Some of them had been on display during the exhibition of students' work the previous fortnight, and Mr Bissell senior—who always looked in on the up-and-coming talent—had left a message that if Anna brought some of her work for closer inspection it was possible that the Galleries might put it on sale.

The Galleries only handled the best in arts and crafts, and it was a rare student who was invited to call, although most of them went in with specimens of their work. Anna was shown into Douglas's office with her caseful of wares. She had had several paintings in the students' exhibition too, but Mr Bissell senior had only been interested in her sewing and embroidery, by which he showed himself a man of taste.

Douglas also knew saleable stuff when he saw it, and he nodded approvingly at a quilt for a child's bed, where friendly-faced frogs played around a shimmering blue pond; at a cushion, exquisitely and exotically embroidered with strange flowers and birds; and a wall panel of an arched window opening on to a vista of hills and trees.

There was imaginative flair here as well as skill, the girl was showing rare promise, and he said, 'They're good, yes,' because Bissells gave encouragement where they could, and a fair deal. 'Very good,' he added, as Anna's rather apprehensive expression gave way to a dazzling smile.

She didn't know why she had been nervous. She had sold almost everything she made and she had intended to set up on her own after she left college, advertising and hoping for orders. But if the Galleries would handle her work then she was off to a flying start and that was wonderful.

Douglas was noticing how attractive she was, with her clear translucent skin and shining eyes. He knew Anna Cameron. He remembered the car crash that had killed her parents, and he admired her courage as well as her talent.

Until now he had always been attracted to dark-haired sultry glamour girls, but he was finding something very appealing in this clear-eyed lissom girl. He was glad she had brought her work to them, because he would enjoy seeing more of her.

She saw what she had always seen in Douglas Bissell, passing him in the street or seeing him in the Galleries, a tall fair handsome young man, and she was glad she would be working with him.

Douglas's mother said he was a born bachelor. He had always had a girl-friend around, but there had never been any signs of him planning to marry any of them. Not that he was a womaniser. A friend of Anna's, who had been a fellow student with her, said that he was more old woman than womaniser, and Anna had denied that fiercely.

As well as his good looks Douglas had a super nature. He was kind and understanding, and although it took him nearly a year to get round to asking Anna to marry him they had been dating spasmodically ever since she began supplying the Galleries with her work.

They had had lunch together when she took in her first consignment, and she liked everything about him. The way he looked and talked, his tastes and opinions. Everything. She had always had plenty of boy-friends around, but there was a feeling of deep quiet strength about Douglas. A girl could rely on a man like him, and although Anna was proud of her independence, and her own strength, the loss of her parents eighteen months before had left a void in her life.

The first time she was asked round to the family home she thought how lucky Douglas was in his home and his family. The Bissells' house was Georgian. So was half the town, but this house still stood in a large walled garden, and none of the rooms had been adapted into apartments. It was still the way it was first built, and filled with period furniture—although the Galleries only sold the work of contemporary artists.

Then there were his mother and father. Mr Bissell was tall and handsome like Douglas, but with a shock of white hair and a few more lines on his face. Mrs Bissell was handsome too, and when Douglas took Anna into the drawing room Mr Bissell was standing by the fire-place and Mrs Bissell was sitting in a red plush chair as though they were waiting.

Anna hadn't known Mrs Bissell at all before then. She'd seen her, but she'd never spoken to her, and Mr Bissell smiled and said, 'Now this is a very talented young lady. We consider ourselves fortunate to be marketing her work.'

He was only half joking, because right from the beginning Anna's sewing sold. But Anna blushed and said how lucky she was that Bissells were behind her, and at the end of that evening—after Susan and Robina, Douglas's sisters, had come in and said hello—she felt that she was accepted as a family friend.

She had been happy all this year. She still wept secret tears for the parents she had lost, but ever since that first day in Douglas's office she had known that she could turn to him if she was ever in trouble. And although he had other girl-friends and she had a lively social life they gradually slipped into regular dating, until they were spending most of their free time together, and there was no one else who really counted for either of them.

On her birthday he gave her a Victorian pearl ring, a heart of tiny seed pearls. He took her out to dinner to their favourite restaurant, to their favourite table in the little alcove, and then produced the heart-shaped box in faded blue velvet.

'Oh, it's beautiful!' she whispered, slipping it on to the third finger of her right hand, but as she lifted her hand to admire it he caught her fingers and shook his head.

'Wrong hand,' he said.

She had wondered when she saw that her present was a ring, but they hadn't talked about marriage, and it was a family joke that he was a born bachelor and he had never denied it.

She loved him, and she knew he loved her, and as he gently removed the ring and replaced it on her left hand she began to smile. 'It looks even more beautiful on this hand,' she said.

They had decided on an Easter wedding. Susan, a year younger than Douglas, had been married a couple of years, and Mrs Bissell still had the guest list from that, and the menus the caterers had supplied. She had them out and was poring over them the night they went back and showed her the ring.

'She loves organising things,' Susan teased Anna. 'You'd better let her do it, because if you don't she'll badger you to death. John and I wanted a quiet little register office wedding, but Mother practically had a nervous breakdown at the idea, and I ended up with six bridesmaids!'

From October to Easter seemed a long time to Anna, but already Mrs Bissell had persuaded her to start embroidering her wedding dress. However, from now until her exhibition Anna would be working on the special picture, the surprise for Douglas. Hearts and sunflowers. A change from roses, because she wanted the colours to be all golds and yellows.

She let herself into the tall terraced house where she

lived, and was half way up the stairs when Joan Pirie
came out of the kitchen into the hall calling, 'That you,
Anna? Did you find anything nice at the sale?'

'Yes, quite a lot.'

'That's good. I'm off to the shops. Anything you need?'

Anna leaned over the banisters, looking down at the
plump little woman with greying hair, in check skirt
and serviceable two-piece, carrying a large basket. Joan's
husband was a schoolteacher, and she did bed and breakfast and evening meal for tourists. She and Anna's mother
had been friends and after the accident, when the small
house where Anna had lived all her life had become
heartrendingly big and empty, Joan had suggested she
sell up and come here, moving into the attic room. It
was full of junk at the time, but they cleared it and
painted it, and now it was a spacious bedsitter-cum-
workroom.

Joan had been a good friend to Anna. Anna had always been lucky in her friends. 'I won't be cooking,' she
said. 'I'm going out tonight. It's Doug's mum's birthday
party.'

'So it is, I forgot. See you later, then.' Joan went off,
swinging her basket, and Anna raced up the two stair-
cases to the attics.

Mr Bissell and Douglas were already watching the
property market for the house where Anna and Douglas
would live when they married, and as the date came
nearer Anna would become more involved in the search.
Nothing had turned up yet, and after she was married
she would probably keep this place on as a workroom.
It was almost ideal—an enormous room, under the
rafters, not sectioned off in any way. She used the bathroom on the floor below, but she had a cooking corner,
complete with small stove and fridge, and a living section
with a studio couch and some of the furniture from her
old home.

The rest was workroom. That was where she liked her

space, so that she could walk around between the wicker baskets each filled with fabrics of a single colour—all the shades of the rainbow—and the baskets with the patterned pieces, for appliqué and patchwork. There was also a desk, a chest containing the more fragile and costly materials, the brocades and silks, and a bureau of little drawers for beads and sequins and shells, anything that might add interest or gleam like gems among the embroidery. Her sewing machines and drawing board were on a huge table, as near as possible to one of the dormer windows. That was the one snag with the room, the light. Bigger windows would have been better. When Anna was doing small intricate work she used electric light too, even in daytime.

Now she tipped out the contents of her canvas bag on the table and began to sort out the pieces for any she might need in the picture. Her design for that was pinned to her drawing board, although when she began sewing it would change and develop. She was always at her most creative with a needle.

She put away the rest of the sale fabrics and had just started tracing the design on to calico when the phone rang down in the hall. She always answered when Bill and Joan were out. Sometimes the call was for her, often it was bed and breakfast customers, and then she would check in Joan's desk diary to see if she could accept a booking.

'Hello,' said Anna. 'This is the Laurels Guest House, can I help you?'

'Any time,' said Douglas. 'Are you free for lunch?'

'I can be. Any particular reason?' The Galleries took orders for her work. If somebody wanted something in a hurry she might not have her picture ready in time for the exhibition, but he said:

'A very particular reason. I like eating my lunch looking at you. And dinner, and supper, and I can't wait to share breakfast.'

Not that it mattered, but that would certainly raise a grin in any of the staff, and she laughed, 'I hope you're on your own in that office!'

'I am on my own, as it happens,' he said. 'But who cares who hears? I love you.'

'I will have lunch with you,' she said. 'Because you say the nicest things.'

She often thought about that lunch afterwards, because it was so ordinary and so happy. There was no shadow on her contentment as she ate her meal and sipped her glass of white wine and laughed and talked with Douglas, proud of him, enjoying it when other women glanced across at their table.

She went straight back home afterwards and carried on working until it was time to get ready for the birthday party. Mrs Bissell was probably about fifty, nobody was saying, but Mother's birthday party was an annual event. Once, Douglas had told Anna, everybody had had a birthday party. His mother liked entertaining, she was a good hostess, but as he and his sisters grew up they preferred to do their celebrating in a less organised fashion, so now it was just Mother's birthday and Christmas Day when the old elaborate parties were held.

Anna was family now. She was Douglas's girl, different from other girls because their wedding was being planned, and as his sisters had told her, she was the first girl he had ever been serious about.

She wore a caftan she had embroidered, deep crushed-strawberry satin glittering with gilt thread and light-catching beads and rhinestones. It wasn't her favourite outfit, she preferred simpler clothes, but in it she was a walking advertisement for her craft. She never wore it without somebody asking where she'd bought it. It brought in the commissions and Mrs Bissell loved it. 'Do wear that beautiful caftan,' she'd said, 'and I'll forgive you if you outshine every other woman at the party. I'd like them all to see what a clever daughter-in-law I'm getting.'

Some of the guests tonight would be strangers to Anna. She didn't move in senior Bissell circles, and neither had her parents. Although she had met most of Douglas's friends this was Mother's party, and Mother's friends would predominate. Mrs Bissell wanted her to shine and so she wore her caftan, and arranged her hair in a high coil with falling ringlets.

Dressing up like this always amused her. She loved the feel and the colours of the garments she created, but when she put them on she felt like a small girl pretending to be someone else. Her make-up was heavier than usual, in keeping, her eyelids gilded and elongated. She looked glamorous and exotic and she knew that Douglas would approve, because she had worn the caftan before and the make-up and he had been all admiration.

While she waited for him to collect her she sewed a few more seed pearls on the bodice of her wedding dress, sitting under the lamp in her 'living room'. She had put away the picture, she didn't want him walking over to the table by the window and finding it, because she wanted to hand it to him, complete and unexpected, and say, 'A present for you, shall we put it in the exhibition? It's a love letter.'

She didn't answer when the phone rang this time because Bill and Joan were home, but Joan came running up the stairs to say, 'It's Douglas,' and Anna got downstairs as fast as her full stiff skirt would allow.

'What's happened?' she asked.

'Could you get yourself over?' He sounded apologetic and she reassured him quickly:

'Yes, of course.'

'My car's playing up. Shall I get you a taxi?'

'Don't bother, I can drive over.'

His home was about a mile away, and it was a fine

evening. She could have walked it in no time if she hadn't been got up like the daughter of Fu Manchu, but it would take only minutes to get into her little car, garaged in one of the row of garages behind this row of terraced houses. 'Be right with you,' she said.

She ran upstairs for her purse and, back on the ground floor, put her head round the door of Joan and Bill's living room to tell them, 'His car's broken down. I'm taking myself.'

'Have a good time.' Joan looked up from the pile of accounts she was dealing with at a little side table. 'Oh, that is a beautiful dress!' she said. 'I think it's one of the loveliest things you've ever made.'

Anna had to arrange her skirts carefully when she climbed into the car, and when she got out, having parked in a discreet corner up against the tall yew hedge. Her car had been third-hand when she'd bought it, and the Bissells' beautiful white Georgian house always made it look clapped out. Tonight there would be some very expensive exclusive cars in this drive, and Anna tucked hers away as though it might get an inferiority complex if she left it exposed.

Douglas was at the door before she reached it, running down the steps to meet her, grinning as he looked across to where she had left her car. She always parked it there, out of the way. It was one of their jokes, Douglas suggesting it needed something to lean on. 'Like me,' Anna would say, and he'd put an arm around her and she'd cuddle up.

He put an arm round her tonight, leading her into the house, where all the lights were blazing and all the party needed were the guests. Anna was rather early. She was family now, and she had to be here when the visitors started arriving, to do her share in welcoming them.

Everything looked beautiful. There was a caterers' buffet stretching all around the dining room, with catering staff at the ready; flowers massed in alcoves, soft music playing.

The Bissells were looking beautiful too, and so right in the setting of this elegant home. The three tall hand-some men : Douglas and his father and Susan's husband, John. Douglas's mother wore a gown of very fine lilac-coloured lace, and his two sisters, with their long smooth fair hair, were dainty and ethereal in flowing dresses.

Anna would have felt more comfortable in something a little less stiff and spectacular herself, but they all crowded around her when she came into the house with Douglas so that she felt at home at once. She knew that they loved her, and how lucky she was that she had been accepted like this.

'Happy birthday,' she said, kissing Mrs Bissell and handing over the little package in her purse. Mrs Bissell had recently started collecting the old bone bobbins that were used by Victorian lacemakers, and Anna had four for her—one with the name 'Emily Ann W.' scratched on it, the others with different initials. Nobody would ever know who the owners had been, but Mrs Bissell seemed to be delighted with the gift, although she would probably have much nicer presents. She was hard to buy for. There wasn't much she wanted that she couldn't go out and get.

Then Anna had to be introduced as Douglas's fianceé to an uncle, an aunt, and a great-aunt, whom she hadn't met before. They smiled at her and she hoped they were approving. They all looked very prosperous, Great-aunt Miriam in particular. She was wearing a dazzling dia-mond brooch on a black velvet gown, and rings that took your breath away; so that Anna wasn't really surprised when she looked down her aquiline nose at Anna's own seed-pearl engagement ring.

Anna loved her ring and this touch of snobbery amused her, but Douglas's great-aunt sounded horrified. 'Not pearls for an engagement ring!' she exclaimed. 'Pearls are for tears.'

Douglas laughed. 'Rubbish, darling, you and your old superstitions!' His fingers brushed Anna's cheek and he smiled at her. 'There'll be no tears in these eyes,' he said softly, and she blinked hard because the extra mascara on her lashes suddenly stung a little.

But even Douglas's great-aunt admired Anna's caftan, and during the evening she found herself discussing it with half the female guests. She knew she was on show, up for inspection, but she joined in the conversation and held her own, and Douglas was proud of her, and it was one of the happiest evenings of her life.

They were asked several times when the wedding was going to be, and once where they planned to honeymoon.

'We haven't decided on that yet,' said Douglas, 'but Anna has a cottage on one of the Scottish islands, we may spend some time there.'

'Oh, how romantic!' gushed the woman who had asked about the honeymoon. 'An island all to yourselves!'

'Well, not quite,' said Anna gravely. 'There are quite a few houses. There's even a pub and a shop—not to mention the ghosts.'

'*Ghosts?*' the woman echoed, and Anna laughed.

'All Scottish islands are haunted, didn't you know that? Everybody who lives up there has the sight.'

Her father had been born on this little island, west of the Western Isles, leaving as soon as he could, and only going back for the occasional holiday. But Anna had spent some of her summers there every year until her grandmother had died five years ago. She had never gone back again after that, it wouldn't have been the same, but she always meant to return some time. St Morag's Isle was incredibly beautiful, and the little terraced house overlooking the harbour had a special place in her heart.

Since her grandmother's death it had been let through

an agency to holidaymakers in the summer months, and the rents that came in were very useful. But during the winter the shutters were put up and it stayed closed and empty until spring.

It would be spring before they wanted it, and when Douglas had asked her where she would like to go for their honeymoon she had said at once, 'What about my cottage? I haven't been there for years, but it's always booked during the summer, so it must be as lovely as ever.'

Sometimes people came back wanting to buy the cottage, but Anna would never sell. So many childhood memories were centred there.

Douglas was doubtful. 'Isn't it rather primitive?' he queried, and she had teased him :

'We're young and strong, aren't we? My grandmother was over eighty when she died and she said that St Morag's was the healthiest place on earth.'

'I was thinking more of somewhere like Bermuda,' said Douglas. 'I'm not much for the rugged life.'

They were still undecided, but it was a delightful problem to have. If they didn't go to the cottage on honeymoon they would go some time, and she would walk through the heather and along the wild coastline with the man she loved.

She linked fingers with him now, as they moved among the guests, smiling because some of them must be wondering what she had that had made Douglas Bissell fall in love with her. She wondered herself, she never stopped wondering, but wasn't it wonderful?

'What are you thinking about?' he asked her, and she hoped she wasn't looking too smug. She said softly :

'How safe I am when you're with me.'

'I'll keep you safe,' he said. 'I'll never let anything hurt you.'

The party finished late and Anna stood with Douglas

saying goodnight to the departing guests. Great-aunt Miriam was staying the night, the other relations were leaving. Douglas and Robina still lived at home, but Susan and John kissed Mother goodbye and ran for their car.

Everybody was running because it was pouring. Some time during the party rain had started, steadily getting heavier until now it was bucketing down. Some guests were making a dash for their transport. Others, older and less agile, were waiting until their cars were brought to the steps, and the ones who had walked here in the fine mild early evening were being offered lifts.

Douglas had intended to drive Anna home in her little car and then walk back himself, but that would have been stupid in this downpour. So when the forecourt was empty she covered herself with a borrowed mackintosh cape, and Douglas held an umbrella over her until she was in the car.

'Get back into the house,' she said, winding down her window and feeling the rain driving in as she leaned out to kiss him. Then she wound up her window again and he stood back, under the big black umbrella, while she turned the car.

It was all the windscreen wipers could do to keep the semi-circle of screen clear. Streets were empty, washed to a shining grey, the street lamps reflected in water as though a river ran beneath the wheels of the car.

She had hardly any distance to go, but driving in these conditions was a strain and she leaned forward, peering with narrowed eyes. Her lids felt heavy and she took a hand from the wheel to rub her left eye, which felt as though she had blinked a lash or a blob of mascara into it.

It was a stupid thing to do, rubbing her eye like that, but she was very tired and she didn't stop to think. She blinded herself momentarily, her eye filling with scalding tears, and as she braked she went into a skid, plunging and swerving, wheels locked, across the treacherously smooth surface of the road, towards the lamp-post that crashed into the little car like a battering ram.

There was no time for fear, hardly any for pain. Pain and blackness came together as the world exploded.

CHAPTER TWO

When Anna opened her eyes the first thing she saw was Douglas's face. He looked so old that she thought at first it was his father, but as her eyelids fluttered she heard his hoarse voice, 'Anna darling, oh, Anna, please!' and then the face was a nurse's and the voice was soothing and professional saying:

'It's all right, Miss Cameron, we're going to be all right.'

Anna believed her. In this warm and floating world there was nothing to worry about. She slept again, and it was the second wakening that was the real one. Again a nurse was there as soon as she opened her eyes and moved her head, but this time she remembered the accident, how her mother and father had died, the monstrous crashing crescendo of concrete and metal, and she tried to scream.

She never knew what kind of sound came out of her throat, she heard them telling her again that she was all right, but this time she had to know, was she crippled? Disfigured?

She was lying in the only bed in a little white room, with a grey square of sky showing through the window, and she whispered to the nurse smiling down at her, 'How badly am I hurt?'

'You were a very lucky girl.' She could move. She ached, it hurt, her arm was bandaged and her body felt awkward beneath the neat smooth sheets, but she could move. Most of the pain was in her head, throbbing somewhere above the hairline, and when she touched her face she shrank at the pain.

'My face?'

'Is going to be fine,' the nurse finished for her, and picked up a hand-mirror from somewhere and held it so that Anna could see.

Of course if she had been cut she would have been bandaged, she wouldn't have felt bare puffy skin. There was some ugly bruising across her forehead and down the side of her face, but the nurse was smiling and promising her, 'In a few weeks there won't be a mark.'

'Thank God,' Anna whispered.

She had been lucky, escaping with bruises and cuts. Some gashes were deep—she had lost enough blood to need a transfusion, she discovered later—but nothing that wouldn't heal. And not on her face where the scars would matter. What were a few scars that you could cover up anyway? When they let Douglas in she smiled for him.

'I should have let you drive me home,' she said.

He leaned over her with infinite tenderness. He had changed into a daytime suit. He was shaved and pale and haggard, he didn't look as though he had had any sleep at all. 'That bloody car,' he muttered raggedly.

'It wasn't the car's fault. What sort of state is it in?'

'It's a write-off. How you came out alive I'll never know.' He picked up her hand, not squeezing it, just holding it between both his, as though to reassure himself it was still warm and living. 'God, we've been so worried about you. We've all been going out of our minds. My mother's under sedation.'

'What an end to the party!' She felt guilty, causing all this trouble. Poor Mrs Bissell—some birthday present! 'What an idiot I am,' she sighed.

He kissed her hand, lightly and gently, and then the unbruised cheek. 'How do you feel?'

'Fragile.' They had assured her that nothing was broken, but she felt that if she was joggled around something might break into small pieces. Her spine perhaps, or the top of her head. She said, 'My head aches like a king-size hangover. Do you think it was the champagne at the party?' and he pretended to laugh at her silly joke because she had only drunk a couple of glasses all evening long. It hadn't been the kind of party to get lit up, not with everybody watching her because she was the girl Douglas was going to marry.

'You had concussion,' he told her.

'Bad?'

'You were out for hours.' She knew by his expression that it had been touch-and-go, and she said:

'Knocked out by a lamp-post?'

'That's right.'

But it was no smiling matter. It meant that the darkness could have lasted for ever, so that she would never have seen Douglas again, never been his wife. When she thought of that she wanted to cling to him and beg him to hold her tight; except that she was in no condition for hugging. 'Does Joan know?' she asked.

'Everybody knows. Everybody's wanting to come and see you.'

It was a pretty little room. A single room. She thought they were all wards these days and she asked, 'What am I doing in here, all on my own?'

'It's a private room.' He must be paying, or his father, and she might have protested if her head hadn't been aching so badly. But at the moment she needed privacy, and not many visitors until she was feeling stronger.

'My headache's a killer,' she said, and grimaced at the word, as Douglas rang the bell to call the nurse, who dispensed some pills that soothed the pain away.

Anna lay quietly that day, grateful for life knowing she had come so near to death. After this she would count every day as a blessing. The only visitors she was allowed that first day were Douglas and his mother, but messages and get-well cards and flowers were handed in, brightening up the little room.

'You're a very popular young lady,' said the nurse, coming in with a large bunch of bronze chrysanthemums from Zoe and Pete, who had been fellow art students with Anna, and Anna was touched. She had good friends, always had had, and when Douglas brought his mother along that evening Mrs Bissell could hardly have been more concerned if Susan or Robina had been in this bed.

She came in smiling then, reaching the bedside, almost burst into tears, and Douglas smiled, pretending to be exasperated. 'What's this, then? She doesn't look as beautiful as usual, but that's only bruising. What did you say when we were deciding who was coming this evening, you or Robina? You said "I'll come with you. I'll help to cheer her up."'

Anna smiled too, but if Mrs Bissell had been under sedation last night no wonder she wasn't quite herself yet, and Anna said, 'Sorry I'm being such a nuisance,' then Mrs Bissell smiled, and sniffed:

'Oh, my dear, you've nothing to be sorry for. We're all just so thankful you're all right.' She had tears on her cheeks and she dabbed at them with her fingertips. 'It was just seeing you lying there,' she explained, 'and thinking——'

Thinking what might have happened, she meant, and that was in all their minds. Douglas began to give Anna messages from the staff in the Galleries, opening the newspaper he was carrying, a local edition featuring a big advertisement about her exhibition next week, and she asked, 'Will I be out of here by then?'

Mrs Bissell answered, 'You won't be staying a minute longer than you have to, and then you're coming home and we're going to look after you until you're quite strong again.'

'That is kind of you.' Anna had fended for herself

since her parents died, with Joan's help in shopping, and in cooking too sometimes. But she would need to convalesce and it was comforting that Douglas's family wanted her.

Next morning Joan came, carrying still more flowers and an armful of magazines, the concern in her eyes belying her cheerful manner. 'You're a right one, aren't you?' she said. 'You've got everyone worried about you.'

Everyone would remember what had happened to Anna's parents. After that Anna's accident would have extra poignancy. 'I must say, though, you don't look too bad,' Joan decided. 'A bit beaten up.'

'Not a single bone broken,' said Anna.

'I'm keeping a front bedroom ready,' Joan gave the nurse the bunch of roses and looked around. 'The florists and the greetings card shops have been doing good business. Anyway, as I was saying, I'm keeping a bedroom ready, and as soon as you're discharged you'll move into that and I'll look after you.'

When she heard that Mrs Bissell had made the same offer she said, 'I thought they might, but you know Bill and I are there if you need us.'

Anna had so many friends. They trooped in, bringing flowers and fruit and books and candies until it seemed she must be supplying half the hospital. She had always been at the centre of things, full of life; and the news of her car crash had shocked them all. They came to reassure themselves that she was still smiling.

She was weak at first. When they got her out of bed she could hardly stand. She sat in a chair for a few minutes, but the room was swimming and her head was aching, and she was glad enough to lie down again and take the painkillers.

For a few days the headache was persistent. She must have had an almighty bump, really shaking her up. When she woke in the night it always seemed to be there as a dull ache, and sometimes it flared during the day so badly that if visitors were around she longed for them to go. The medical staff reassured her that this was part of the shock to her system and she had every kind of tests and X-rays, all of them proving that she was going to be as fit as ever again.

Everyone was wonderfully kind, but after a few days she wanted to get out of this bright little room, full of get-well cards and smiling faces. She was beginning to feel depressed, an aftermath from the euphoria just after the accident, although she kept reminding herself how lucky she was.

For the first time in her life she was taking sleeping pills. If she hadn't she wouldn't have slept, she was doing nothing to tire herself, but she would stop that as soon as she got out of here, and when Dr Doyle decided at last she could leave it was the best treatment of all. He was the doctor in charge of her case, a man of few words, with the plump face of a bad-tempered baby, double chin and turned-down mouth. And half-spectacles well down on his nose. The staff were all in awe of him. If you asked a question more often than not you got your head snapped off, and Anna had asked several times when she could go home. 'When I'm ready to discharge you,' he'd told her. But when he said, 'I see no reason why you shouldn't leave us tomorrow,' she looked at him in an entirely new light and decided he was probably likeable after all.

Douglas and Robina fetched her. She was nearly as good as new, all the cuts healing, and make-up camouflaged the bruises on her face. She could have gone back to her apartment, she didn't need this tender treatment, although it was pleasant to have Douglas's arm around her, helping her along the corridor and out into the car; and Robina hovering like a solicitous sister.

Anna sat back in the passenger seat, repressing a little

shiver—this was a different car and Douglas was with her and she was always safe with Douglas—and said, 'I feel a bit of a fraud, getting all this fuss.'

'You had a nasty accident,' Robina told her. 'You had to have a blood transfusion.'

'Yes, well, I don't remember anything about that, but I'm all right now so long as nobody starts thumping me.'

'Do as you're told,' Douglas joked, 'and you won't get thumped.'

They passed the Galleries with the big notice in the window 'EXHIBITION, Anna Cameron'. The strawberry-satin caftan should have been the centrepiece in that window together with a few more pieces to lure the passer-by into the shop and into the exhibition. But instead there was a circular black skirt that Anna had made and appliquéd with huge scarlet poppies.

She had turned to look as they passed. She knew the exhibition had opened, and Robina said, 'We'll go to-morrow.'

'I suppose,' said Anna. 'The caftan I was wearing—was it——?'

'If you look at that you'll know why you needed a blood transfusion,' said Douglas grimly, and she knew that she didn't want to see it. She would never ask about it again.

They gave her Susan's old room, with white and gold furniture, and a thick white wall-to-wall carpet, and she said, 'After all this luxury I'm going to find it hard to adjust to my attic again.'

She was joking, but Mrs Bissell, who had gone up to the room with her, said quite seriously, 'I see no reason why you shouldn't stay here until the wedding,' and Robina asked,

'Why don't you? I miss not having a sister to talk to last thing at night.'

They were so kind, so loving, but Anna missed her

attic. Her work was there, her things, and until she married Douglas and shared a home with him, that was the home that suited her life-style best. She was here as a guest, grateful for their kindness, but soon she must go back and get her life-style together again.

Not that she didn't enjoy her stay. Mrs Bissell had a resident housekeeper and a daily and Anna was forced into the role of lady of leisure, which was super for a few days, as good as a holiday. Although everybody seemed to think she should be taking a holiday before she got down to work again.

She was paler than before and Douglas regretted that he couldn't take time off from the Gallery to take her somewhere warm and sunny. If he could have done she would have gone, and although she didn't need any more rest she half agreed to phone a friend somewhere and go for a visit, but she wasn't committing herself to going on holiday because she was feeling better and stronger every day.

Her first trip out was to the exhibition, which was bringing in the orders and gave her self-esteem a lift, and she had several outings with Robina. She was really getting to know Douglas's sister, who was twelve months older than Anna herself but seemed younger, perhaps because she was the baby of the family, and still didn't quite know what she wanted to do with her life. She was supposed to be working in the Galleries on the side but often stayed at home and helped her mother on various committees organising coffee mornings and garden parties and sales of work. All for good causes, but she seemed to envy Anna, who had to earn a living and was making a small name for herself in the process.

'It must be fantastic to have your talents,' said Robina, fingering the beaded bodice that Mrs Bissell had brought over. 'I used to get quite good marks for art myself. Not outstanding, but goodish.' She smiled wryly. 'But even if I'd gone on to art school I wouldn't have been good enough for the Galleries, so there didn't seem much point in it.'

Anna didn't know what to say to that, except, 'I must be getting back to work.'

Joan had phoned that afternoon and said that Mrs Bissell had called and collected the wedding gown, and told Joan that she expected Anna would be staying with them at least until Christmas.

'Will you?' Joan had asked Anna. 'I can understand that it's nice over there, and you're marrying Douglas soon, but we should miss you, and what about your work and everything if you're just going to sit around making your wedding dress?'

By now Anna was fit enough to go home, and when Douglas came back that evening she told him, 'It's been lovely here, being spoiled by everyone, but I must go home tomorrow.'

'You're sure about that?' He looked concerned, and then grinned. 'I guess you are. My mother's going to nag you about it.'

Mrs Bissell was becoming very fond of Anna. Douglas's previous girl-friends had always been flashier and self-centred, not at all suitable. Anna was a nice girl, no trouble at all. Mrs Bissell was sorry she was leaving them, but it was finally agreed that tomorrow, after breakfast, Douglas would take Anna back to her attic bed-sitter before he went on to work; and tonight Anna was packing her case.

'I'll miss you being in here,' said Robina, putting the wedding gown bodice back between tissue paper in the box. She looked up, her face grave, then she smiled. 'You're going to be a very beautiful bride,' she said.

The scars were healing, fading. Each night Anna examined them and now the dressings were off, all but her arm which she had probably thrown up to protect her face. The stitches had been taken out before she left hospital and she wouldn't need plastic surgery; she was hardly going to be marked at all.

The headaches had gone. Sometimes she woke in the morning with the faintest hint of one, but that could happen to anybody who had been through the ordeal she had just weathered.

Everything was wonderful again, and tomorrow she would start on the orders that had come in during the exhibition. She was looking forward to that. While she was here she had started embroidering one of Robina's blouses, just for something to do. It needed another hour or so of work on it, and it was downstairs in the little parlour. She might remember it in the morning, or again she might not, so it would be better if she fetched and packed it tonight. If she left it behind it might never get finished, and that would be a pity.

She went downstairs, the lights were still on, and the door of the drawing room was a little ajar. She heard Mr Bissell's voice as she crossed the hall, saying, 'She's determined to go back, there's nothing you can do about it, and she'll be all right now.'

They must be talking about her. Robina was upstairs, but Douglas and his father, and possibly his mother, were still sitting over late drinks, and talking about her leaving tomorrow. She went on tiptoe. As she was under discussion it might be a little embarrassing if they heard her crossing the hall outside the door. Then Douglas said:

'I know there's no danger now, but when I think what a near thing it was. . . .'

Her blood felt colder and she stood still; it was chilling to be reminded how close she had come to death. 'It doesn't bear thinking about,' he said. 'Anna, blind!'

Blind? Was that what he said?

'She isn't going blind,' said his mother. 'You know

she isn't. The tests showed that—you know they did.'

'I would still have married her.' He sounded on the defensive, and his mother said soothingly :

'Of course you would. She's a sweet girl, a lovely girl.'

'But it would have been a hellish life,' said his father, and Anna cringed away, back from the door, softly creeping up the stairs.

When she was inside her bedroom she gasped for air like a poor swimmer coming up from the depths, choking, floundering. *Blind?* The word exploded in her head for a moment the pain came back fiercely. The headaches were shock, she had never thought they might be symptoms of damage. All through the searching tests she had never been afraid that she might go blind.

She would rather be dead than unable to see colours and shapes, all the wonderful things that made up the world. She was shaking, huddled on the side of the bed, staring around the room as though the lights could go out and the night could last for ever.

But it wasn't going to happen. 'No danger now,' Douglas had said, and they had kept the fear from her, these kind, caring people. She had been grateful to them before, but now she could never be grateful enough. Because if she had known what kind of razor's edge she was on she would have gone crazy in that little room with the cheering cards and the vases of flowers.

She prayed a fervent prayer of thanks. She had thought she was lucky that the scars on her body were fading, how much luckier she was that her eyes were still letting in the light.

She left the bedside lamp on all night, because when she switched it off the darkness frightened her. She had always quite liked lying in bed with the lights off waiting to fall asleep, and watching the grey shapes form as her eyes grew accustomed to the dark. But tonight she switched the lamp on again, quickly, and got up and went to her case and took a couple of sleeping pills. She hadn't touched them since she left hospital, but tonight she needed them if she was going to get any sleep at all.

She wished she hadn't gone downstairs. She would have been happier never knowing that she had not only escaped death, but living death, because Mr Bissell was right, blind life would have been hell. The horror of it gave her nightmares, in spite of the drugs, and when she woke in the morning she jerked up in bed staring wildly around her.

For a moment she thought she had dreamed it all, and then she remembered, and remembered to be thankful because there was no danger now. The last tests had shown that, and the headaches had gone and she could see as well as ever, every fibre in the coverlet, the smallest detail in the matching floral wallpaper. When she got up and stood at the window she could see the lawns and the hedges and pick out a bird in a tree. She had always had perfect eyesight, and she still had; and she didn't need reassuring, so she wouldn't tell them what she had over-heard, that would only embarrass everybody.

But when she went downstairs into the breakfast room, and Douglas and Robina and Mrs Bissell all smiled at her, she stood in the doorway blinking away tears, and Douglas asked anxiously, 'All right, darling?' as he came across to kiss her good morning.

'Fine, thanks, I'm just thinking how marvellous you've all been to me.' Her smile was unsteady and they all said that they had done nothing, they'd loved having her here, they were going to miss her badly. 'Come and have some breakfast,' said Robina, pouring out tea.

These sort of breakfasts would be a thing of the past when Anna got back to her attic. Here the table was laid with a blue and white cloth, and blue and white china, marmalade and honey in pretty little pots, coffee in a percolator, tea in a Wedgwood teapot. There was nothing rushed or makeshift about breakfast here, and afterwards Mrs Bissell and Robina kissed her goodbye, although she would probably be seeing them again tomorrow.

On the way to her home the car passed the accident spot. The lamp-post showed signs of repair, the concrete had been patched and it was still slightly askew. She looked at it as they drove by and Douglas said, 'It came off better than the car.'

'I came off best of all, didn't I?'

He smiled, 'Yes, you did.'

'I love you,' she said.

'I love you.' That was why he would have married her even if she had been a blind woman.

She looked out through the car window, and every detail in the busy street was thrilling because she might have been sitting here and seeing nothing.

Joan waved through a ground-floor window as the car drew up outside the house, and she was in the hall when they came through the front door. She gave Anna a hug and Douglas a warm smile. 'All right, are you?' she asked Anna.

'Never been better,' said Anna. 'I've had a marvellous rest.'

Douglas had to get to the Galleries. He was carrying Anna's case and he went ahead, and Joan said to Anna, 'I'll see you in a few minutes. Go careful on the stairs.'

Did Joan know her sight had been in peril? Anna wondered. She went up quick and sure-footed after Douglas. He had the key, she hadn't been here since her accident, everything she wanted had been fetched for her, and he opened the door and left the key in the lock.

Everything was more or less as she had left it when she had set off for the birthday party. The room had been tidied, but only to the extent of putting magazines and books tidily, clothes into cupboard, and laying the table in the living section with items for a cup of tea.

There was a new pot plant—a camellia with a label 'Welcome home, Joan and Bill', on her work table by the window, and a couple of letters that had arrived by this morning's post.

It felt good. Homey. She had the orders that the exhibition had brought in her handbag, and she was eager to start work. She took off her coat, dropping it on a chair, and Douglas put down her case and put both hands on her shoulders. 'Don't overdo it now,' he said. Her satisfied smile and her darting eyes had told him she was figuratively rolling up her sleeves. 'And I'll expect you around one o'clock for lunch.'

They were having lunch together. Anna could have talked to him then, if she had to discuss it, but she said suddenly and impulsively, 'Doug, my headaches, those awful headaches I had at first—you know they're gone now, but did they mean anything?'

'They meant you had a bad time,' he told her gently, and she said bluntly :

'Did they mean my eyes might have been affected?'

He hesitated and tried to look away, but her clear gaze held him and he admitted at last, 'At one time they weren't sure.'

'They're sure now?'

There was no hesitation when he said, 'Oh yes,' and from the relief in his voice and face, she knew how much strain he had carried before the final verdict was given. She reached up to touch his cheek, patting it in comfort and apology for what she had put him through, and when he asked, 'Why are you suddenly wondering about this?' she confessed :

'I overheard you and your parents talking last night. I came downstairs to get something I had to pack.'

The colour deepened in Douglas's face, mottling his

cheekbones. 'Oh, my God!' he groaned. After trying to
protect Anna all along the line it must be sickening to
hear that she had learned about the awful thing that
might have happened to her by accident, by a fluke. He
looked appalled, as though he couldn't look at her, and
then he said huskily, 'It doesn't matter what you heard,
I love you.'

'I know,' she smiled at him. 'And I heard your mother
say that the tests showed it was all right, but I'd never
realised there was any risk until then. You promise me
I'm all right?'

'Yes.' He repeated it, 'Yes. You can talk to Doyle if
it will make you happier. We kept it from you, but
you're in no danger now. None.'

She tried to say, 'I believe you,' because she did believe
him. But the words came out, 'I believe you, but I
would like to talk to him,' and when Douglas said, 'I'll
see if we can get him,' she said:

'Thank you,' meekly because she shouldn't be causing
any more trouble. But it had been such a shock, hearing
what she had heard, that there had to be a tiny residue
of doubt and fear in her mind. Once Dr Doyle told her
everything was all right she would be quite reassured. On
a matter like this he would have to give an answer.

Downstairs in the hall Douglas dialled a number, gave
his name and asked if it was possible to speak to Dr
Doyle. 'We're in luck,' he said to Anna, and a few moments later, 'Good morning, doctor, it's Douglas Bissell
here. Please would you tell Anna that her eyesight is fine.
She's just realised there was a time when we were worried about it and she needs your reassurance.'

'Hello, Miss Cameron,' came the doctor's voice. 'How
are you?'

'Wonderful,' said Anna a little breathlessly, 'but I've
only just heard that I might have ended up——' She
couldn't say 'blind' but the doctor did.

'You could have ended up blind, but you didn't, and there's absolutely nothing wrong with your eyes now. Nothing wrong with you either, is there?'

She laughed, agreeing, 'Thanks to all of you.'

'No more skidding around in cars, then.' He sounded as disapproving as though she made a habit of it. Then he wished her goodbye, and she hung up and turned to Douglas, who kissed her and said:

'One o'clock for lunch.' She was going to the Galleries, then they were going out to lunch together, and she went back upstairs now without a worry in the world and her only problem what to start working on first as soon as she had unpacked her case.

She would have liked to finish Robina's blouse or start on Douglas's picture, but she had to get through the orders and she decided to spend the next few days on a small quilt, ordered for a child. They wanted a Siamese cat on this, and had left a photograph of Sheba, the family pet, sitting on her favourite red cushion. The blue, slightly-crossed eyes glared out, and Anna began to draw a copy of the photograph, from which she would make the pattern.

Joan came and chatted a while, glad to have Anna up here again. 'That's an evil-looking beast,' she said, looking at the sketching pad.

'One little girl loves her,' said Anna. 'Beauty's in the eye of the beholder.' She would stitch two blue sequins to catch the light in Sheba's eyes and give life to the patchwork satin-stitched cat. 'Talking of eyes,' she said, 'did you know that they weren't sure about my eyes after the accident?'

'Oh *no*!' Joan cried in horror, knowing what failing eyesight would have meant to Anna.

'It's all right,' Anna hastened to reassure her. 'It got better, whatever it was. The nerves somehow, I suppose. There's no danger now. I was lucky all round, wasn't I?'

It was lovely walking along the streets going to the Galleries. This was the first time she had been out since the accident and her exhibition was showing. She heard a couple of women admiring the goods in the window, which gave her a glow, although she resisted the temptation to say, 'I made them, I'm Anna Cameron.'

Douglas was on the phone when she looked into his office, so she went into the exhibition room and chatted to Helen Whitehead, a smart-as-paint young woman who was in charge there. Helen was just off to lunch herself, so she joined Anna and Douglas, at Anna's invitation, and most of the meal they talked about work.

After lunch Anna called on some of her friends who lived or worked around the centre of the town and said, 'Hello, I'm back again.' What with that and the shopping for provisions most of the afternoon had gone before she was climbing the stairs to her room again, her arms around a very full carrier bag.

She had to put down the carrier to open the door, it wasn't locked, and as she stooped to pick up the bag she saw Mrs Bissell sitting over there on the divan.

She gasped because she hadn't been expecting anyone, then she smiled and said, 'Hello, this is nice. I've been shopping and I called in to tell one or two folk that I'm back at the old address. Have you been here long?'

'About half an hour.' Mrs Bissell didn't sound too happy.

'And you haven't even made yourself a cup of tea!' Anna deposited her carrier on the draining board, and picked up the kettle. There was something odd in the way Mrs Bissell was just sitting there. If she had been here for half an hour you'd have expected her to turn on the radio or find something to read, but she hadn't even taken off her gloves. She was just sitting, bolt upright in the middle of the divan, looking so upset that Anna's throat tightened.

The first thing that came to her mind of course was her own escape from blindness. That was the panic she had to hold down while she was asking, 'Is anything the matter?' Although this couldn't have anything to do with that. They might have kept the full facts of her physical condition from her at first, perhaps not knowing had helped her recovery, but it would be criminally unethical of the doctor to lie to her now. Her eyes were safe, so what was making Mrs Bissell so anxious?

Whatever it was Mrs Bissell didn't seem to know where to start. She sat twisting her hands, biting her lip; while Anna waited, fear rising in her in spite of her efforts to control it. Then Mrs Bissell said jerkily, 'What must you think of us? Last night—Douglas told me you heard us talking——'

Only a few words. Nothing to explain why Mrs Bissell's conscience was troubling her, nor why she was saying, 'Ever since I've been remembering what was said, and I simply had to come and explain.'

'Please don't.' Anna didn't want to hear any more, and Mrs Bissell wasn't very coherent.

'Douglas would have married you if——' she stammered and gulped and tried again, 'if you——' and stopped again.

This time it was Anna who said the word, 'If I had gone blind?' and Mrs Bissell nodded, lips compressed and trembling. 'It might have sounded as though there was —well, his father——'

So Mr Bissell had had reservations about a wife who would have been a burden on his son; that was natural enough, Anna could understand that. 'It doesn't matter,' she said. 'It didn't happen,' and Mrs Bissell smiled for the first time.

'No, thank God,' she said. 'And Douglas would never have let you down.'

'I'm glad about that.' Anna realised she was still holding the empty kettle and said, 'Tea? Shall I get you a cup of tea?' but Mrs Bissell was on her feet looking for her handbag that was just beside her.

'I must go home. I had to talk to you, but nobody knows I'm here, and I must get back.' She hesitated, clutching her handbag and said pleadingly, 'You won't mention that I was here?'

'Of course not. And there was no need.'

There was no car outside, Mrs Bissell must have walked. She must have been worried, and Douglas had been tactless to mention it to her. Anna wouldn't have done, because everything was fine now. There was no danger and she had overheard nothing, except that her eyes had been at risk, and Douglas would still have married her if she had gone blind.

More was said, obviously. If she had stood and listened outside she would have heard that the family hadn't all been waiting to welcome her from the beginning. It seemed at first Mr Bissell had advised Douglas to think twice before committing himself to a girl who might be appallingly handicapped; and Anna would have been a manic-depressive if she had lost her sight. Who wouldn't? It was about the worst thing that could happen to anyone even if her eyes had only deteriorated a little, giving her poorer eyesight; her work would have suffered, and she loved her work. It would have taken a long time to reconcile her to giving that up or becoming second rate. She would have been a drag on any man and no one could blame Mr Bissell for saying the future would have been hellish.

She was glad she hadn't listened. She didn't want to know what else was said when they'd thought they were alone, and she was upstairs in the white and gold room that had been Susan's. Mrs Bissell had walked the half mile here to tell her that Douglas loved her, and that was all she needed to know. And of course what the doctor had told her that she wouldn't be a burden on anyone.

When she had traced the picture of Sheba, the Siamese cat, she went through her baskets for scraps of material, black velvet and white satin, and began to cut them into shapes, tacking them to the canvas base. The picture would be stuffed, to stand out in 3-D, and then saddle-stitched on to the quilt.

The seed-pearl bodice was on the table in the 'living-room', the boxes of pearls and beads and needles and fine silk thread were beside it. Anna hadn't worked on that since the night of her accident, nor seen it till Mrs Bissell brought it along yesterday. That was her wedding dress, and they were talking about the wedding again now. Susan and Robina, and Zoe, were going to be brides-maids, but were still undecided about the style of their dresses. Since Anna had come out of hospital they had talked about wedding dresses, but not while she was in hospital.

She hadn't noticed that before. Other visitors had. 'You'll be O.K. for your wedding, anyway,' but the Bissells hadn't talked about marriage. They'd talked about friends and work and the weather and the news and how well she was recovering, but they had never discussed wedding plans. Not once. Not even Mrs Bissell, who might have looked on Anna's enforced inaction as an ideal opportunity to go through the guest lists, and that kind of thing.

When they took her home, presumably as soon as the final results on her eyes were out, Mrs Bissell had said, 'Why don't you stay here till the wedding?' and while she had been in their home, growing stronger every day, there had been a lot of marriage talk.

She couldn't blame Douglas's parents if they had been uneasy at the prospect of a blind daughter-in-law. She could have hardly blamed Douglas if he had been afraid for himself as well as for her. Douglas hadn't talked about the wedding either while she was in hospital, but she was sure that he would have stood by her if the worst had happened.

Well, she had been sure. She hadn't doubted it until Mrs Bissell came along saying, 'Douglas would have married you ... Douglas wouldn't have let you down,' as though Anna might have heard something that could have shaken her faith in Douglas.

She had stopped working. Her hands lay idle on the scraps of material and her mind raced back to this morning and the expression of horror on his face when she'd told him she had overheard them talking last night. When he'd said, 'It doesn't matter what you heard, I love you,' he had sounded ashamed for a moment, pleading for understanding.

Or had he? She couldn't be sure. And she never would be sure whether he loved her enough to have shared a dark future with her; or whether, if her sight had failed, she would have been jilted. Gently, almost lovingly. The family caring for her like good friends, helping her in every way, but the marriage always being postponed.

She would never know for certain and she had to believe her own instincts. Of course she trusted him, and he loved her, and at Easter she would marry him, thankful for his love and for her eyes that could see him. She picked up the velvet again and the scissors and went carefully around Sheba's pointed ears.

It would have been stupid to dwell on doubts, so she concentrated on her work, revelling in the delight of creating a strokeable little cat, with slanting shining eyes, for a little girl's bedspread.

She had a couple of callers before Douglas came. Zoe and Pete, who had a stall in the indoor market selling lamps and shades, and wax candles in all shapes and colours which they made themselves. Pete was big and bearded, Zoe was nearly as tall but lanky, wearing jeans pinned at the waist where the zip had broken, and a tight purple sweater that looked as though it had shrunk in the wash.

They had come as soon as the market closed bringing a bottle of home-made wine which they poured into tumblers to toast Anna's return to health and to her bed-sitter. When Douglas arrived Pete was sprawling on the divan. Zoe was cross-legged on the floor, and Anna still stitching Sheba and had moved to the lamplight by the living room table.

Douglas didn't have much in common with Zoe and Pete, but they had always been Anna's friends, and he gave them an affable, 'Good evening', when he came in. No, he said, he wouldn't have any of their home-made wine. He kissed Anna and sat down heavily on the end of the divan just beyond Pete's feet and told them, 'It's been a hellish afternoon.'

Zoe and Pete sympathised with him; there hadn't been much doing in the indoor market either, although Douglas's difficulties had been centred round an afternoon with the accountant working out VAT returns.

Anna sat sucking her finger tip where her needle had slipped and pricked. She didn't do that often, but when Douglas said, 'It's been a hellish afternoon,' she had been startled because he had sounded just like his father last night, saying, 'But it would have been a hellish life.'

Douglas and his father were alike, in looks and in voice, and she was almost sure it was his father who had been speaking when she stood outside that door. Whoever it was they were right, of course; she hoped it hadn't been Douglas.

He was leaning forward now, asking what she was doing, and she held up Sheba, coming on nicely on a backing of calico, and he smiled, 'You haven't lost your touch.' But I could have done, she thought. I wouldn't have been an asset then to you or the Gallery, and the bitterness of that shocked and surprised her.

She wasn't quite herself again yet. That was the root of the trouble. Being involved in a car crash had brought back her parents' accident. The shake-up had been mental as well as physical, and discovering the cracks in what had seemed the solid support of the Bissells had undermined her security and contentment.

She desperately wanted to have everything the way it used to be and during the next two weeks she worked hard, too hard and too late perhaps, but often when she was with Douglas and even when they were closest and she should have been feeling like the luckiest girl in the world the thought would insinuate itself—would you have wanted me still if I had been stumbling behind you for the rest of my life, instead of able to run on ahead?

She hadn't sewn any more seed-pearls on her wedding dress, although the date still stood and there was no question at all that the wedding might not take place. Mrs Bissell was busy with catering and guest lists, Douglas and his father were still checking on property. Anna asked Douglas whether he had seen any houses while she was in hospital and he said that he hadn't. Most of his spare time had been spent at the hospital. 'We didn't know what kind of a house we should be needing, did we,' she said, 'if my eyes had failed.'

Douglas scowled, 'For God's sake don't be so morbid!' He sounded almost angry, and she had apologised, 'Sorry, it was just a thought.'

She kept the thought to herself that if her sight hadn't recovered they might not have been sharing a house—that was why he had stopped looking for one; but in spite of everything she could do it stayed with her, a little festering doubt of which she was ashamed.

She came home late one night from Douglas's home,

and took out the seed-pearl bodice again. During the evening Robina had produced a picture for the brides-maids' dresses and Anna and she had discussed how it might be adapted to suit not only Robina and Susan, with their petite figures, but also the angular Zoe.

The two girls had been alone in the drawing room at the time and Robina had suddenly said, 'Oh, I'm so glad everything's going to be all right! It would have been too awful if anything had stopped you and Douglas getting married.'

'Like me going blind, you mean?' said Anna softly, and Robina begged, 'Don't talk about that,' but she didn't deny it. Anna hadn't talked about it any more and after she had said goodnight to Douglas she had taken out the seed-pearl bodice, although it was nearly eleven o'clock at night.

She should be doing something about this if it was going to be part of her wedding gown, and she turned on the bright lamp and started stitching. It was going to be so pretty with its floral motif of tiny pearls and tinier silver beads, and she loved embroidering. She expected it to calm and relax her, although it was bedtime she didn't feel ready for bed. But she must have been wearier than she knew because suddenly her eyes blurred as though they were brimming with tears, and she had to blink them clear again.

She sat very still, her blood turning to ice. That had never happened before even when the headaches were at their worst. And the headache was coming back. She could feel the first pulsing throbs beating in her skull, so perhaps the doctors were wrong, and the tests were wrong. Perhaps her eyes were failing, she *was* going blind.

She looked down and saw the embroidery shaking in her hands and put it aside and clenched her hands to-gether, gripping so tight that her engagement ring cut into her finger, forcing herself to be calm and reasonable.

This hadn't happened before because she had never worked such long hours before. Tonight had been the first evening since she started work again that she had sewn on until supper time. She was trying to finish the orders from the exhibition, but she wasn't a hundred per cent fit yet from her accident, and her head wasn't aching. That had been pure imagination, but it just showed the state she was in.

She should have taken advice and taken a holiday when she came out of hospital. She needed to get right away and do some calm quiet thinking.

She was all confused. She didn't really know what she wanted any more, whether she trusted Douglas or not, even whether she wanted to marry him or not.

But suddenly she knew where she wanted to go. To St Morag's, to the island. Suddenly it seemed that the answer to everything would be waiting for her there.

CHAPTER THREE

DOUGLAS thought Anna was mad—not because she had decided to take a holiday, but when she told him where she was going. It was November, he reminded her, as though she might have forgotten. This time of year it would make more sense to fly out to the sunshine rather than get herself stuck on a bleak little northern island. And in a house all on her own. Who did she know on St Morag's anyway?

'Nobody,' she admitted. Six years ago, that last summer, she had swum with a boy and a girl who lived, like her grandmother, in one of the row of houses behind the harbour wall. She had known her grandmother's friends and neighbours, but six years is a long time. They might remember her, but she doubted if they would recognise her.

'Well, I can't get away,' said Douglas irritably, 'but I suppose you can get somebody to go with you. There's always Robina.'

'I don't think Robina would appreciate the island,' said Anna. On warm summer days, perhaps, but even then St Morag was rather too spartan for Robina's tastes. In any case Anna wanted to go alone. 'I'll be all right,' she insisted.

'Why?' demanded Douglas.

At one time her grandmother had seemed the wisest woman in the world, wiser than her parents or teachers, although Mary Cameron had never travelled further than fifty miles from St Morag's in her whole life. Anna remembered how the tangled problems of childhood and adolescence had smoothed away when she was on the island. Life had seemed simple and sweet there, and that was how she wanted it to be again.

'I don't know why,' she said, 'but I'm going,' and Douglas grumbled, 'You don't seem to be the same girl since your accident.' She couldn't deny that, but now she had made up her mind she was longing to go back to the island. Nobody could have stopped her.

It was almost like it used to be, packing for her holiday, except that this time she put in winter clothes, jeans and sweaters, and an oilskin, and she borrowed a sleeping bag from Zoe. Bookings for the cottage stopped at the end of September, but she rang up the agents to make quite sure no one was still in residence, and was assured that the shutters were up and the house would be empty all winter long.

'It hasn't had its springclean yet,' she was warned. Before the holiday season started the firm that handled the bookings arranged for repairs and repainting, but it wouldn't worry her if the place didn't look bandbox-neat. It never had in her grandmother's day. There was a supply of oil and fuel there, she was told, and a few tins of food, but if she planned to stay any length of time she would have to make arrangements about that.

'Of course,' she said happily, remembering the little all-purpose shop on the island, and the hens and cows; but she would take some food with her.

Douglas was still perplexed, frowning as he kissed her goodbye and put her on the plane for Glasgow, on the first stage of her journey.

She stayed in Glasgow overnight, and next day took a much smaller plane to the Isle of Carra, and down in the harbour a man with a fishing boat agreed to ferry her the last eight miles to St Morag's. As her baggage was taken aboard he asked her, 'Staying with friends?'

'Yes,' she said, because she didn't want to go into details. She didn't want to talk, and she sat in the bows

of the boat, her face turned towards the grey shape of
St Morag's rising from the sea.

The spray and the salt smell were familiar, and the
cries of the seabirds, but she had never come here cold
and late before. When she was a child she had always
been met off the plane from Glasgow. In later years a
boat had been waiting in the harbour at Carra, and when
they came to St Morag's her grandmother had been out
on the jetty, scanning the horizon.

Nobody was on the jetty today and fog was beginning
to rise from the sea. Anna paid the boatman who asked,
'Your friend is expecting you?'

'Yes.' He helped her carry her luggage up the rock
steps, and she was glad she didn't have far to go because
she was chilled to the bone. The cottage looked fine,
although she didn't stand outside examining it. It was
painted white with a white door, and white shutters over
the windows, and the paint might be peeling a little, but
not so that you'd notice on a late afternoon in November
with fog rolling in from the sea.

She opened the shutters and the door, and put her
suitcase and bedroll inside; then collected the box of provisions and brought that in. She went quickly, although
there didn't seem to be anyone about. She couldn't bear to
tell anyone just yet that she was Mary Cameron's
granddaughter; she might have burst into tears if she
had.

Her first sight of the cottage by the torch in her handbag was depressing too. It had been so cheery and welcoming in her grandmother's lifetime, with bright light
streaming in through the windows or the lamps burning
mellow and warm. And always a white cloth on the
table and a meal being served. Well, it had seemed that
there was always food ready.

The old brass lamp still stood in the middle of the table,
which was bare now, and she shook it gently, hearing the

swish of oil, searching in her bag for matches. When the lamp glowed it was the old room, but not the same. All the clutter of ornaments had gone.

Her mother and father had come to the island when they were preparing the cottage for summer letting, but most of the breakables that had no practical use had been shared among friends and neighbours. Anna hadn't wanted anything, for the same reason that she had refused to come back to the island all these years. She had wanted to remember it as it was, even pretending sometimes that her grandmother was still here, waiting for her.

She warmed her hands now over the globe of the lamp, and moved the wooden-backed rush-seated chairs a little way from the table so that they looked less orderly. She put the rugs in the places they used to be, and shook up the cushions on the sofa. There was a Davy lamp hanging from a hook in the kitchen ceiling, fairly shiny and new, that had replaced an earlier lamp. She would fill it tomorrow, but now she would have something to eat and settle down on the sofa for the night.

The mist was curling and swirling against the windows as she pulled the curtains together. If the wind had been rising she would have gone outside and closed the shutters again, but the walls were thick and the warmth from the lamp was already taking the chill from the small room. Tomorrow would be soon enough for going outside.

She was exhausted. That was one of the reasons she was here, because she had overtired herself; but the journey had been a strain and she suddenly felt that she she couldn't have walked another step, and if this little house had been even half way up the hill she could never have dragged herself there.

There would be no hot food until she got the stove going, so she ate cheese and buttered biscuits, and drank from a carton of long-life milk, sitting at the bare table, slumped in a chair. She had brought the sleeping pills with her, in case she had difficulty falling asleep, but she need not have worried about tonight. It was all she could do to keep awake long enough to get out of her clothes and wipe her hands and face with a cleansing pad. Then she turned out the lamp and climbed into the sleeping bag, pushing cushions under her head.

She was here at last, on the island. If she closed her eyes she might drift back to her childhood days, resting on the sofa sometimes while her grandmother stitched away in the lamplight. Or upstairs, watching the clouds float over the moon, remembering the old wives' tales that were part of the magic of the isles. They all had their kelpies and hogboons, but only St Morag's had the dark men.

Off Spanish Sands, on the other side of the island, a galleon had sunk in the storm of the Armada, blown there from the battle, to founder and sink in the deep dark water. The legend of the dark men had given Anna delicious thrills of terror as a child. During summer storms her grandmother would tell her she could hear voices, calling over the wind and the rain and the crash of thunder, if she was quiet and listened. She was safe, so long as she never answered, and she had believed she heard her name called in the wind, but she would have died sooner than utter a word.

She wondered if the children here still kept their hands over their ears during the storms, and if the brother and sister who had been her summer playmates until she was fifteen still lived at the end of the terrace. They would be into their twenties now. Everybody would be older, and tomorrow she would meet some of them again.

She fell asleep to the sound of the sea and she woke to a grey morning and looked through the window across the little harbour. The sea was choppy, it looked very cold, and the harbour was empty. Anna had never seen it like that before. There had always been boats, bobbing on the water or drawn up on the shingle.

Perhaps the fishing boats were out, and in wintertime some must be under cover. But the harbour wall was broken in front of this house, and when she moved close to the window, looking to left and right, there seemed to be no sign of life at all. Except for the seabirds.

She pulled on a coat over her pyjamas, slipped into shoes, and opened the front door, her heart racing and her mouth dry because there was not another open door. Some of the houses were shuttered, no smoke rising from the chimneys. Others were derelict, with gaping holes instead of windows or doors.

Anna remembered that this had seemed to be a busy little harbour, there had been people in every house, and now there was nobody. Of course it was winter now, but they hadn't been summer visitors, most of them hadn't. Some perhaps, but most of them had been like her grandmother, living here summer and winter.

Where had everybody gone? Where were the people?

She dressed as fast as she could. The road from the harbour led to another street just behind these houses. There were more houses there, and the store. The MacDonalds lived there, he had a boat called the *Ellen Louise*; and Miss McPherson had kept the shop.

As she stepped out of the house she noticed the thin bitter sea grass growing between stones beneath her feet, and she began to run through the gulley. But when she turned to look down the road, towards the shop, a scene of desolation reached her.

Like the harbour houses these were shuttered and empty. The shop was closed. The name painted over it had almost weathered away. A couple of cottages just beyond had a gaping hole in the roof. That was where the MacDonalds had lived, six years ago, in the far cottage.

Six years was a long time. Although he had seemed hale and hearty Mr MacDonald had been old. The old could have died, the young must have left. Some of the houses were summer lettings, you could pick those out, like her cottage; and there were other houses on the island that probably still had folk living in them all year round.

Perhaps it was just down here that there was nobody left. The man who brought her over had asked if she was staying with friends, so there had to be somebody somewhere. Unless they'd gone without telling him. Unless this was like one of these science fiction TV films and she was the last woman in the world.

A gust of wind had her coat flapping about her, and she cupped her hands round her mouth and shouted, 'Hello, anybody there?' and felt the emptiness echoing all around.

Now she must go back to the cottage and get dressed, eat something, and take a walk. She would go to every house, she would find somebody, and if she didn't she wouldn't panic because she had come here to be on her own. She had chosen the loneliest place she knew, the closest to nature.

Birds were still here, and the seals. People booked the cottage for their holiday year after year. If she had wanted to sell the agents could have found her a buyer. It was a beautiful, magical island. But the visitors had all come in the summer and this was wintertime, and she walked back trying not to hear the echoes of her own footsteps following her.

The harbour was a ghost harbour, and as soon as she got inside the cottage she checked the oil supply. That cheered her. She found a five or six-gallon plastic drum of paraffin nearly full in the kitchen, which meant she could keep the lamp going at night. She hadn't fancied sitting around in the dark. There was a Calor gas cooker

—she didn't know how much was left in the container, so she must use that carefully. But outside the fresh water tank was full and there was a bag of coke and a bag of wood in the lean-to shed.

The food she had brought with her would last several days, and there were a few tins in the kitchen cupboard. She hadn't made any arrangements for getting back, but everybody at home knew where she was. She had told them she was staying for a couple of weeks. After that somebody—Douglas, of course—would come looking for her. In the meantime, if things got desperate, she could light a beacon on a hill. That would be seen sooner or later and bring over a boat.

There was island blood in her, she should be able to cope. She laid the fire before she went out, and used a ring on the cooker to boil just enough water for a cup of coffee. She wasn't hungry, but she took an apple and a bar of chocolate with her.

A hill rose steeply from the harbour and she passed the remains of another cottage, and what had been the island pub. It was a long time since that had served anybody; the windows were holes, and green lichen moss grew on inner as well as outer walls.

In the old days Anna had explored the island countless times from end to end, every hill and cove and cave, walking for miles across the open heathland. She knew where every house and croft was, and she began trudging from house to house now, but everywhere tracks, and what had been rough but serviceable roads, were overgrown. She reached about a dozen houses in all; three had shutters up, the rest were falling apart.

She met nobody, not even a dog, although a small flock of sheep were grazing. There was no sign of a shepherd, no other sign of life. People might be where she couldn't see them, of course, down in coves, or out in boats, or just out of sight; and there were several houses she would leave till tomorrow. But it was becoming likelier all the time that she was quite alone here, and that would have frightened her to death if she hadn't been preparing herself for it from the first moment she had looked out on the empty harbour this morning.

Douglas would have had a fit if he had realised that the island was deserted over the winter months, and of course she wouldn't have come if she had known. But now that she was here, and perhaps nobody else was, she had to adapt until somebody came to fetch her off.

It was exciting as well as scarey, and as the wind streamed through her hair and the salt air tingled her skin she felt a kind of exultation. She was queen of this country, and her eyes were as keen as a seabird's. She could see for miles. She might make wall panels of the island when she left. She might sketch while she was here.

She would get back to the cottage in daylight and settle herself in comfortably for the night, and not think about being caught out in the open in darkness, because once she admitted that this situation could reduce her to a gibbering wreck she was half way there. She would keep telling herself that it was wonderful, beautiful, that nothing had changed except that the people had gone, and winter had sharpened the wind with a savage edge and coloured the sea a sullen pewter.

She passed a cottage in ruins as she went down to the beach under the cliffs where the cormorants nested in summertime. The path down a gentler slope—on which the cottage stood—had vanished under bracken, but she picked her way, stopping when she was struck by the thought of what a sprained ankle could mean. Then she shrugged; once she gave way to over-caution she could end up scared to take a step, so she would just be sensible and avoid crazy risks.

This had been one of her favourite places. When she

used to come here the nests seemed to be in every crevice in the cliffs and the air was always full of birds. She had climbed the cliffs then, but this afternoon she sat on the beach and watched the waves creaming into foam on the glistening black rocks.

There were boats out there, perhaps some of them would come back to the island. If she lit her beacon it would be seen, but she had wanted solitude.

She would never have more peace for working out her problems, and she began twisting the ring on her finger, because that was her problem. Did she love Douglas enough to marry him?

She had had no doubts before the accident, and she must love him or she wouldn't be wishing he was with her now. But as he said, he wasn't much for the rugged life. The idea of him, in his city clothes, sitting on this beach beside her, made her smile. And then tramping back to the deserted harbour and trying to make a meal out of the food she had brought. Douglas was fussy about food. Douglas was fussy, Zoe said. Zoe was the one who had described Douglas as an old woman, but that was because he declined to sell her home-made candles in the Galleries.

It was very quiet. The wind had dropped and the waves were breaking sluggishly on the shore. Even the birds were making hardly any sound. Anna had never been alone like this before. She wondered how long it would take to get used to it, and if they could see her from that boat on the horizon.

They couldn't, of course, but she waved, and shouted 'Hello there!' as loud as she could, but her voice was drowned by a cacophony of squawks and cries, and a great flapping of wings as disturbed birds took off from their perches on the cliffs.

And a shout. Unmistakably somebody yelled, and Anna jumped up and stared up. A man was coming down the cliff, while all around him birds swooped and flapped their wide white wings.

He seemed sure-footed enough, but she was glad to see him jump the last few feet to the shore, although when he straightened up he turned and glared at her.

He had a thatch of black hair and a great beak of a nose. He was wearing jeans and a fisherman's sweater, and she didn't know him. She didn't think he had been here in those old summers.

He didn't look pleased to see her. He was demanding, 'Where the thunder did you spring from? You nearly got me knocked off the bloody cliff!'

'I'm sorry,' she said, and her explanation seemed reasonable enough to her. 'I didn't see you up there. I didn't expect anybody to be birdwatching this time of year.'

'Then who were you shouting at?' His eyes were as dark as his hair, as his eyebrows, and he was still scowling.

The boat that was a speck on the skyline, actually, although she had really shouted to break a silence that was becoming awesome. She said, 'Anybody. I was beginning to think there was nobody else on the island.'

'Well, now you know there is,' he said, and he gave her another glance and strode off, along the beach to the slope and up that to the heathlands. Anna watched him all the way, but he didn't look back once, although with the scarcity of company around you'd have thought he'd have at least asked, 'Which is your house?'

Unsociable swine! Not that she wanted company, especially his kind. What was his kind? she wondered. He might be an ugly customer, although somebody who was birdwatching up a cliff seemed unlikely to be violent or hiding from the law. She hoped.

He had *looked* violent. But if he'd been sitting on a narrow ledge up there, believing there was no one else for miles, it must have been hair-raising to hear a shout and have every bird on the cliff face leaping off and flapping its wings.

If there was one man around there were probably other folk too. The friends the boatman had thought she was joining. More than likely there would be a boat and certainly food, and although she wouldn't bother them it was a relief to know that in an emergency she could ask for help. The man hadn't been friendly, but he was human.

Last night she had thought she had neighbours all around. She had slept soundly in the row of empty cottages, but tonight when she closed the door she knew she was alone down here. It was light still and she stood at the window, and the desolation of the empty harbour made her shiver.

She didn't want the island to herself. Not the whole island. If she met the man again she would apologise again for yelling, and ask if there were any more people here.

She put the lamp in the window, so that if any boats did come in they would see this house was occupied and someone might knock on her door. She went upstairs before night fell. There were just the two bedrooms, with a big bed in one and two small iron bedsteads in the other. There were blankets in a tin trunk, but the bedrooms looked chilly and she decided to stay with the living-room sofa.

She closed the door on the creaking old staircase and busied herself getting a meal of corned beef and baked beans which she ate very slowly in front of the fire. Then she took out her sketch pad. She never went anywhere without that, and she wanted to draft a rough idea for a wall-hanging inspired by the old tale of the storm and the galleon. Several pages of the pad were covered with hearts and sunflowers, sketches for her I-love-you panel for Douglas, and she sighed as she turned them over. She might have brought that with her, and made it while she was on holiday. It would have been a present to take back, but there was no inspiration for golden hearts and sunflowers in this wild and lonely place.

Nobody knocked on the door and she saw no boats come into harbour and, before she climbed into her sleeping bag, she went outside and closed the shutters. She didn't linger over that. She banged them sharply together, slipping the latch across, and almost ran back into the house.

She was undecided about sleeping pills. Sound sleep wasn't going to be so easy tonight, although she had walked for miles today, but as she tipped the two white tablets into the palm of her hand she decided she was being too hasty. She might sleep peacefully enough without them. If she was still tossing after an hour or so then she could always get up and take a pill.

She did toss for a while, but the knowledge that there was at least one other person on the island made a difference, although she had no idea where he was nor who he was. She was not quite alone, she told herself, and at last she tossed into slumber.

With the shutters drawn her first glimpse of day was a thin bright line in the middle of the window. She had to open the door to find out what kind of day it was, and it looked less bright outside. Navy blue clouds were filling the sky, and it had been raining. It was the kind of day to stay indoors, but what could she do indoors once she'd filled the lamp and brought in the fuel? If she went out there was always a chance of meeting a neighbour.

She had brought oilskins and gumboots and she didn't mind getting wet. She had the fire going, damped down with some peat she had found in the lean-to, and she wanted to visit Spanish Sands.

She hadn't reached it yesterday, it was straight across

the island, where the great jagged rocks were, facing the open sea. It was easy to imagine ships being battered to pieces there. Others had sunk, before and since the galleon, and this was the kind of day it might have happened when ships were powered only by sail.

Anna was about half way between the harbour and Spanish Sands when the rain began falling again, and after a while she took off her headscarf because its dampness was more uncomfortable than the rain on her hair. If there had been anybody at home in the cottage she might have turned back, but there was only the empty harbour and the empty house, and she had to tire herself or she wouldn't sleep tonight.

Besides, the Spanish Sands wall hanging was kindling her imagination. She wanted to fix the shapes of the rocks in her mind, and this was a day to blow the worries away. She had no thought of failing eyesight, or failing strength, as she battled through the heather against the wind and marvelled at the colours of massing storm clouds.

When she reached the cove she stood with her back against a great wet rock that the sea would cover at high tide, and watched the wind-lashed waves. The weather was getting worse, which was obliging of it, because this was what she had wanted—a storm off Spanish Sands.

She closed her eyes and listened for thunder, and lightning came as a white flash through her eyelids. She could smell the storm, she was absorbing the atmosphere through her skin, the texture and the colour of it, all turbulence and danger.

'Hey there!' she heard, and she opened her eyes, and the man who had nearly fallen off the cliff was at the water's edge. He must have walked from behind the rocks. He waved, and Anna had a moment's reluctance before she lifted a hand and waved back and called 'Hi!' in answer.

He was all in black, with the black sky and sea behind him; and as he came towards her her lips twitched as she reflected—they don't come much darker.

When he reached her he smiled, white teeth in a tanned skin, and remarked, 'You do keep cropping up, don't you?'

'I was thinking the same about you.' Now that he wasn't scowling he had a rather attractive face, and Anna found herself smiling too, with a suspicion that she should be recognising him. Today he seemed vaguely familiar.

'How long have you been here?' he was asking her.

'On the island? Two nights now.'

'Where?'

'Down by the harbour.' Rain was gleaming on his thatch of hair, and his face glistened with it. She was every bit as wet herself, and when he suggested:

'Come and have a bowl of soup, you're a long way from home,' she said gratefully:

'That would be nice.' It would be nice to find a friend and she could do with some hot soup. He must live in one of the houses she hadn't reached yesterday, one did overlook Spanish Sands. She had questions to ask, but they could wait until they reached shelter, and she followed him up from the beach.

The weather didn't seem to be bothering him; he wasn't even wearing an oilskin. He walked into the rain as though it was his natural element and he would later shake himself dry like a dog.

They were making for the house above the cove. Shutters were still up at the front windows, but they went round the back and into a kitchen, with a range that glowed red through the bars when he opened the door. It was a much bigger kitchen than her grandmother's. This had been a farmhouse, she remembered, there had been a smallholding here, and she said, 'I'm glad you've got a house. I'm glad you don't come up from the sea.' When he looked puzzled she smiled, 'Don't you know the story of Spanish Sands?'

'Oh, you mean the galleon and the dark men?' Perhaps he was an islander, he seemed to know it well, and she said:

'My grandmother believed every word. I'm Anna Cameron.' Water was pouring off her oilskin, making a widening puddle on the flagstoned floor, and she got out of the coat. 'Could I hang this up somewhere?'

He took it from her and put it on a hook in the little passageway and said, 'Get out of your shoes as well and make yourself comfortable.'

'Thank you.' It seemed that her oilskins and gumboots had been a good protection. Shed of them she was fairly dry, except for her soaking hair, and he tossed her a towel that had hung over the range.

She began to rub her hair, the warm towel felt good, watching him unlacing sodden boots and peeling off socks. She expected him to go and change into dry clothes, but when he opened a cupboard, took out a tin of soup and poured it into a saucepan, then stood over the hotplate leisurely stirring, she said, 'Shouldn't you be getting out of those clothes?'

'They'll dry.' They were already steaming slightly from the heat of the stove. 'We get a lot of storms this time of year.'

He was swarthy dark, Spanish-dark, and she laughed, 'You wouldn't be Spanish, would you?'

'Only on my father's side.' He turned to grin at her. 'My mother was from Glasgow. That's where I was born.'

'Honestly?' She thought he was joking, but he nodded, although he went on smiling. 'Well, that's a right coincidence,' she said. 'You should feel at home in Spanish Sands.'

'I do. My name's Paul Peralta.'

'I really am extremely pleased to meet you.' Anna was towelling her hair vigorously. 'Is there anyone else here?'

The table was only laid for one, so when he said, 'No,' she wasn't surprised.

'I mean on the island.'

'No,' he said again, and she gulped and he asked her, 'How come you didn't know that?'

She began to twist the towel round her head like a turban as she tried to explain, 'I landed when it was starting to get dark and foggy and I didn't look around me, I just went into my cottage—it's right on the quayside, just at the top of the steps. I didn't realise till next morning there was nobody in the other houses. It's six years since I was here. There seemed to be a lot of people six years ago.'

'Well under a hundred,' he said. 'There are still a few in the summer.'

'I know that.' She tucked in the ends of the towel, adjusting it firmly on her head. 'My cottage—it was my grandmother's—is let during the summer months. I haven't been here since she died. I didn't realise how things have changed. Where have they all gone?'

He poured the soup into the bowl on the table and into another that he took out of the cupboard, sat down himself and waited for her to sit too. The bread looked fresh, home-made, and she helped herself and tucked into the soup, finding that she was ravenously hungry.

'Most of the young folk have been leaving for generations,' he told her, between spoonfuls of soup. 'These days mod cons are necessities. In the last few years the middle-aged moved to the mainland too, and a few of the old ones. The rest died out.'

Anna was glad her grandmother had died while she still had neighbours, that she slept quietly here among the stubborn old ones, because no one would have moved Mary Cameron alive.

This was the recurring pattern of deserted islands, but she still said, 'I can hardly believe it. St Morag's seemed so busy. I used to come up every summer.'

'How old were you when you last came?'

'Fifteen.'

'You probably never noticed that some of the houses were standing empty.'

She hadn't. Her grandmother was still here, her grandmother's neighbours on the quay, the brother and sister she had played with. Although she remembered now that there was talk of a job in Australia for their father, and she said sadly, 'I only know that everyone was friendly and the sun always seemed to be shining.'

There had been summer storms, with flashing lightning and thunder rolling like the guns of the sunken galleon. There had been soft rain, blustery days, but St Morag's had always seemed a safe and lovely place.

'You were never here in winter?' Paul Peralta asked, and she shook her head and he said, 'Winter is another world.'

The storm raging outside was like no summer storm, and she had to walk right across the island to get back to her cottage. She had never been in this house before and it took a moment to recollect the name, then she asked, 'Didn't the McGregors used to lived here?'

Paul was finishing his soup. 'It belongs to their nephew now. He rents it to holidaymakers in the summer, but I prefer winter myself.'

'I'm so sorry.' She made a mock-contrite face. 'You expected to have the whole island to yourself? I do apologise.'

'Forget it.' He leaned over his empty soup bowl, misquoting the old cliché, 'This is big enough for both of us,' and again it seemed that she ought to be recognising him.

'Did you used to come up here years ago?' She tried to imagine the face six years ago. He looked in his middle twenties. That beak of a nose and thatch of black hair must have been with him almost from childhood. He wouldn't have looked much different six years ago.

'Once or twice with Neil,' he said.

She couldn't remember Neil, who must be the Mc-Gregors' nephew, but of course she could easily have seen Paul and Neil down in the harbour, or walked past them somewhere on the island, and forgotten except for this faint memory that stirred whenever Paul smiled.

He was smiling now, into her thoughtful face. 'Any more soup?'

'Please!' It would save her own small stock of food, and it had a good hearty meaty flavour. She let him pour another generous helping into her bowl.

'What brought you here?' he asked.

'I just thought I'd like to see the place again.' He put the saucepan back on the stove and she left her spoon in her bowl of soup. When he looked back at her she was twisting her ring, round and round, without even realising it until he enquired:

'On your own?'

An engagement ring meant a lover, but she hadn't brought a companion on her sentimental journey. She said quickly, 'He couldn't get away,' and grimaced a little. 'He said I was crazy to come, this time of year.'

That showed what a sensible man Douglas was. The sort of man whose advice should always be taken. 'Of course neither of us had a clue that the place was un-inhabited,' and she wondered how long it would be before Douglas found out.

'Not quite,' said Paul. He reached across the table and took her hand and looked at her ring, and she felt a flutter of panic. She was alone, she didn't know this man at all, but the panic was not so much fear as excitement. Something was struggling inside her, but she didn't draw her hand away.

It was almost as though she did know him and had

come back here to find him, and he had every right to
be holding her hand and there was no ring on her finger.

'Does he know the story of Spanish Sands?' asked Paul.

'No.' She hadn't discussed the island very much with
Douglas, except that he knew she owned the cottage and
she had suggested they come here for their honeymoon.
She had never told him the legend that if a girl answered
the call of one of the dark men, from the galleon off
Spanish Sands, she would never be free again. Afterwards
he would follow her always, a shadow in the shadows,
and when he called again she would have to answer.

They smiled at each other, and she would never forget
the way he looked, the bony face with the high cheekbones, strong, wild somehow. The fact that he didn't
seem like a stranger, but someone she knew and had
always known, made him all the more dangerous. The
rain rattled on the window and he asked:

'Will you stay?'

'No.' She drew back her hand, but she could still feel
his fingers curled around hers.

'It's a long walk back and it's a biggish house.'

'Mine's big enough.' Anna was going home, to her
empty cottage on the ghost quay, but she wanted to stay
here and she was twisting her ring again, because she
must be out of her mind to want to stay. 'How long will
you be here?' she asked.

He shrugged, 'I don't know.'

'What are you doing?'

'Living cheaply. Free lodgings.'

'But what are you *doing*?' she persisted. 'Do you have
a job?'

'I write.'

This could be a good place for a writer, but she'd never
heard of him, and when he went on, 'I've also been
salesman, labourer, actor, barman, fisherman—you name
it,' she said:

'And layabout?'

The grin was neither admitting nor denying. 'I've got this idea for this play,' he told her.

'Tell me about it.'

'Not just yet.' Later he would tell her. They would talk about it over meals, or walking across the brown bracken and the winter heather. 'Any more questions?'

'I don't think so.' She wouldn't ask what he had written. He was probably unpublished, that was why he was here, where he could live cheaply in free lodgings. And he wasn't deeply involved with anyone or he wouldn't be here alone. Then she thought of an obvious question. 'Except, do you have a boat?'

'Yes.'

'Oh, good.' That meant she was not marooned, she could get away.

'And how do you go about earning a crust?' he asked gravely.

'I sew. Embroider. Make things. Pictures, quilts, fancy work on clothes. I thought I might do a Spanish Sands wall panel when I go back. That's what I was doing down there, thinking about that, when you called to me.' Their eyes met again, clear amber-brown and brown so dark they looked black. 'Are you one of the dark men?' she asked, gaily, although her heart was pounding hard enough to hurt.

'Of course.'

A flash of lightning came. It wasn't the first, the storm was almost overhead, but that arrived so on cue that they both burst out laughing, and Anna got up and went to the window.

'You're not afraid of storms?' he asked from the table.

'No.'

She heard him laugh. 'A daft question to a girl who'd traipse in this weather right across the island. Come and watch it over the sea.' She thought he meant outside, and she might even have gone outside without shoes or coat when he took her arm, pressing the soft skin above her elbow. But he led her to one of the front rooms, shadowy behind the shutters, and she stood in the doorway of the room while he went outside.

The light came suddenly through the window and she caught a quick glimpse of him in the rain. This place was like her grandmother's. Old-fashioned furniture, a three-piece suite in this room in a dark green moquette, a well-worn green and rust carpet, a biggish table up against the wall, and several small chairs. McGregor furniture, now being used by visitors, who came for their summer holidays. And Paul who had an idea for a play and was lodging here free.

The house had a commanding view of Spanish Sands. From this window you saw right out to sea to the rocks, and over all was the black dome of the sky, lit by the flashing of forked lightning. When Paul came back Anna said, 'I think I'm being over-ambitious. I can't imagine this stitched into a wall panel.'

'Are you good?'

'Terrific,' she said. 'I sew like nobody's business.' Some day she hoped to be terrific, she only considered herself goodish as yet, and she would never have said anything so big-headed to a stranger. Only to someone who would understand what she meant.

'One day,' said Paul, and he put an arm around her and they stood together, watching the storm. Then he unwound the towel she had wrapped around her head and dropped it on one of the green moquette armchairs, and she shook her still damp hair loose and rested her head on his shoulder, her cheek against the rough wool of his jersey.

'I wish you'd change into some dry clothes,' she said.

'I'm all right.'

'Get out of this anyway.' She plucked at the sweater. 'It feels like wet wire wool.'

He stripped it off so that he was naked to the waist

and put it on top of the towel, then drew her close to him again and her lips brushed his shoulder and it tasted salt.

His body was cool and smooth, dark as his face, an all-over tan, and it wasn't strange to her. She felt she could have described every muscle and blemish : the small mole on the shoulder, the ribs showing under the taut skin, the feel of his spine if she had run her fingers down it.

They didn't talk all the time they watched the storm, and they watched it play itself out, the seconds lengthening between lightning and thunder until both died away, and the rain went with them. Then Anna said, 'I must go home.'

'I'll light a fire,' he tempted her. It would be cosy in here, in the parlour, with a fire burning in the old black grate.

'Another day,' she said.

'There'll be that.' Looking down at her, he cupped her face in his hands. His smile was sweet and familiar, and she could see herself reflected in his eyes as though she was part of him. 'There'll be tomorrow,' he said.

There was a cold bowl of soup on the kitchen table, which he insisted on warming up again and watching her eat. How was she for food? he asked, and she told him :

'I brought some—not much. I thought the shop was here, and I could get eggs and milk.'

He went into a pantry and began to put tins and packets into a small cardboard box. There was a loaf of bread on top when he carried it out and placed it on the table and Anna said, 'Thank you. Who made the bread?'

'I did. That should see you through till tomorrow.'

'Lucky I met you.'

'I hope so,' he said.

She finished her soup and got back into gumboots and waterproof. Her wet headscarf was still screwed into a damp ball in her pocket, but her hair was tangled like seaweed anyway so the wind and the rain couldn't do her much harm on the way back. In any case the rain seemed to have blown over, although the wind screamed around them all the way.

Paul went with her, in the same boots he had put to dry in front of the fire, but wearing a Windbreaker this time. He carried the box of provisions and they followed what had been the road across the island, passing abandoned farms and derelict houses.

Anna asked at the first house, 'What happened to the McKenzies?' and Paul said:

'He died. She went to live with a married son.' That was it, every time, death or departure. Sometimes some of the family came back in the summer, but their real homes were far away, and before long she stopped asking. There was only sadness trying to see St Morag's as it used to be, looking for what was no longer here.

Paul walked fast, even with the cardboard box of food in his arms. Like a natural athlete, which he'd have to be if he went climbing cliffs where a slip could smash him up and no one around to run to the rescue.

Anna kept pace easily enough, she'd always been a strider. Douglas used to catch her arm to hold her back and say, 'Steady, no rush!' and she chuckled at that now, and Paul gave her a sidewards grin, dark hair flopping over dark eyes.

'Share it,' he said, and she told him a half truth.

'I was remembering that yesterday I wondered what would happen if I turned my ankle.' She could still do that, the heathland had almost overrun the road. 'So I decided to keep to the smooth ground,' she explained, and he grinned:

'You didn't, though, did you?'

'I forgot about it.' And she had known this morning that he was somewhere on the island. 'I must have known

I was going to meet you on Spanish Sands,' she said.

'Of course.'

She wondered if he was joking or if he too had this feeling they were meant to be on St Morag's together, because she was easier striding along beside him than she would have been with any other friend. She had friends, men as well as women, who were close and dear to her, but Paul was the right one for this place.

Even Douglas would have been hopeless, impossible. Douglas was the man she was going to marry, but she couldn't imagine him walking through the wind, carrying her provisions, and not complaining bitterly; while Paul was in his element. Even if another storm hit them it wouldn't worry Paul.

The sky was still dark. If it should start raining again Anna could hardly refuse him shelter, or turn him out to trudge the return journey to Spanish Sands. If he did have to stay the night he could have one of the upstairs rooms and his choice of the blankets from the tin trunk. But things were not moving at that rate, even if she did feel they had known each other for years! So, on second thoughts, she would take an upstairs room, and bolt the door.

They came down the hill past the shell of the little inn towards the empty harbour. As they reached the row of houses just before the quay Paul told her, 'The shop opens two days a week in midsummer.'

'Miss McPherson?'

'She went to join her sister, the teacher, when her sister retired. They're in a bungalow now. Someone comes here from a shop on the mainland.'

There were still no boats in the harbour, and even the shelter of encircling cliffs couldn't prevent the wind whipping up the sea so that the waves broke high against the harbour wall, breaching it where the breaks were. They walked close to the houses as the waves almost reached her cottage door. The spray did. It was wet on Anna's face as she opened the door.

'Where's your boat?' she asked, slipping inside the cottage and beginning to wish she had a house a little further from the sea.

'In McNab's Point.'

That was a cove not too far from Spanish Sands, but clear of the rocks, a tiny natural harbour, the obvious place, with cliffs that provided comparative shelter. 'She's only a little outboard motor,' he said, 'but she'll get you back.'

'Not yet.' She wouldn't care to be doing the crossing on a day like this, that strip of water was notorious for cross currents and submerged rocks. She said, 'Not until the weather improves.'

He was in her tiny kitchen, checking her cupboard, putting the food out of the cardboard box on to the shelves. 'We're in for a bad patch,' he said.

'Oh dear!' She sounded very cheerful, then she asked with a touch of apprehension, 'Do the tides come in much higher than this? With the harbour wall down am I likely to find myself floating out on the sofa one stormy night?'

'You'd be safer at Spanish Sands,' he leered, and she laughed.

'So you say. I think I'll take my chances here. I can always move upstairs.'

'Foiled again! Now, are you all right for oil?'

'I filled the lamp this morning, and the one in the kitchen.'

'And the fire's O.K.' He looked around, a searching glance, missing nothing, then he drew her to him and kissed her on the lips, sensuously but so swiftly that she had no chance to resist or return the caress. 'I'll see you tomorrow,' he said.

'Yes, all right.' She was still standing on the same spot

when he passed the window. The abruptness of his departure had surprised her, and left her feeling a little disappointed. She had expected him to stay longer than this.

It was daylight still, there was a long lonely evening ahead, and she took a couple of instinctive steps towards the door to call him back. Then she checked herself, because if he returned she might find it hard to turn him away before night fell. And after night fell she might find it impossible.

CHAPTER FOUR

ANNA washed her hair in the rainwater, towelled it again, then left it to dry, tossing loose. Tomorrow she would tie it back, as becomingly as possible. She hadn't expected to bother much how she looked on the island and the wind and the weather would strip off any surface glamour fast enough, but at least she'd start the day with her hair soft and shining.

She lit the lamp early. It was already shadowy in here under the overcast skies. She could borrow oil for the lamp now if she needed it, so there was no need to economise too stringently. Then she opened her sketchbook again and began to make a sketch of Spanish Sands.

She had been to the cove many times and seen the rocks like jagged teeth, with the waves crashing over them. But in summertime the sea hadn't reached so hungrily nor so high and the lights glittering on the water had been sunlight, not lightning. It was wilder now, a cruel and savage place.

She sketched a whole fleet of galleons, with sails and pennants billowing in the wind. And the dark men. One dark man with Paul's face.

Anna found that so absorbing that she went on drawing Paul's face, smiling to herself, thinking that she could sew him in profile so that it was a recognisable portrait. She had never done a portrait before, except for animals. She had done nursery rhyme characters on children's quilts, but she had never tried to copy a face, and it would be tricky unless there was some very distinct feature. Paul's hawklike profile, for instance, and his shock of dark hair.

When she got back she would—but then she stopped, and grimaced, imagining Douglas's reaction if she returned from St Morag's and started working on the portrait of another man from a sketchbook full of drawings.

She turned a page and tried to draw Douglas, but his features weren't as strong as Paul's. The result seemed smudgy and blurred; and at last she shut the book on them both and sat at the window watching dusk falling over the deserted harbour.

The uneven edges of the broken wall stood out in black silhouette. The wall could no longer hold back the sea when the tides were high. There was nothing to hold back the sea, and she remembered how Paul had tasted of salt. He had been walking on the shore, near the water's edge, wet with the spray as well as the rain, and she began to smile again because she had called him down from the cliff and up from the sea. So it was a good job she wasn't superstitious or she might be wondering now if she had acquired herself a demon lover.

He was very attractive, very at home on the island and able to cope with winter here. An ideal companion to be marooned with, and she wondered what Douglas and her friends would think if they knew the kind of situation she had landed herself in. Most of them would say she was the lucky one. But not Douglas, nor his family.

'Sorry,' she said, as though Douglas was in the room with her; and if he had been it wouldn't have placated him at all to see her smiling.

She closed the shutters with night thickening around her, and settled down to read a paperback thriller that one of the holidaymakers had left behind in a sideboard drawer. She didn't want too grim a tale as she was all on her own, and when she found that it was about a hideous moronic killer, and he was hunting down the girl, she put it aside hastily. It was bad enough being all alone down here without listening for shuffling, snuffling noises outside.

She had some of the bread Paul had given her for supper, crusty and fresh and delicious, and with cheese and pickles she was probably asking for indigestion and nightmares. But when she snuggled down in her sleeping bag she soon drifted into sleep. She woke next morning feeling happy and rested. They said that meant pleasant dreams, even if you couldn't remember any of the details, and perhaps it did.

She yawned and stretched and started to put on her shoes and coat to slip outside and open the shutters, hoping for fine weather. How lovely it would be if the sun was shining. It wasn't raining, but there was no sign of sun. The breeze was cold and Anna shivered and hurried back indoors. When there were neighbours living in the other houses it would have been less bleak on these bitter days. The houses huddled together would share each other's warmth, and a word, or a nod and a smile, would be as comforting as another layer of clothing. She was shivering from loneliness as much as cold and she couldn't wait for Paul to arrive.

She filled the kettle from the hand pump over the stone kitchen sink and put it on the Calor gas ring, then she washed quickly and dressed in a thick sweater and jeans and leather boots. She was using a lot of moisturiser on her skin, and lipstick, and she fastened her hair back with a green ribbon, the colour of her sweater. She had a head-hugging woolly hat that should keep her ears warm, and she would probably wear her oilskins again. Nothing was better for keeping out the wind.

She began to fry bacon. When Paul turned up she could cook some for him, even if he'd had breakfast he'd be hungry again after the two-mile walk. She was taking it for granted that he was coming and that they would spend the day together. He'd said he was working on a play, but he'd also said, 'See you tomorrow.'

He hadn't said where he'd see her, so as soon as she'd finished her breakfast she would start walking towards

Spanish Sands to meet him. If she had to go all the way there it wouldn't matter, she had no plans for her day. Perhaps he worked in the mornings. If he did perhaps she could prepare a meal for both of them.

She opened the kitchen window a fraction, cooking fumes were filling the tiny kitchen and the small living-cum-sleeping room, then she sat down to eat her bacon and drink her cup of instant coffee. She was about half way through both when she heard 'Anna!' so faintly that she could have been mistaken, it might only have been the wind. But she jumped up and ran out of the house, along the harbour wall to the gulley that led to the hill.

As she came into the gulley she saw Paul. The hill rose straight ahead and he was coming down towards her. He must have called her name from the top, as soon as he could see her house, and the grey day seemed to brighten, as though she had only been half awake before.

She started to run up the hill and he began to run down, both on a collision course straight for each other until they met with an impact that knocked the breath out of them, so that they stood there laughing and swaying, arms around each other. Although Paul was far from being the most handsome man she had ever seen Anna had never met anyone who could make her feel so good, just standing here, laughing, holding on to him and looking at his face.

It would have been awful to have been quite alone on the island, in spite of all the pep talk she had given herself. It was fantastic luck to find somebody like Paul, but this went deeper than relief. She didn't stop to analyse it, she only knew that at this moment everything seemed possible, in a release of strength and power that made her feel as beautiful and as free as a bird.

She gulped and asked, 'Have you had breakfast?'

'Yes.' He was looking at her as though she was the best thing he had seen this morning. 'Have you?'

'Some of it.'

They linked arms and walked down the hill. A keen wind was still blowing over the grey waters, and she asked, 'Do boats ever come? I was thinking I might have to light a distress beacon.'

'They don't usually come, except in the summer months, but that would have fetched someone.'

This was a holiday island now. In winter nobody came, and Douglas was going to be horrified when he found out. Anna bit back a smile. 'Douglas is expecting me to send picture postcards back,' she said. 'He'll give it about a week and then he'll start wondering what's happened to me.'

He might phone up the agency that did the summer lettings and they'd tell him that so far as they knew most of the houses were closed down. But they wouldn't know for sure whether there were other people on the island. Douglas wasn't likely to be worried enough to travel up here unless she overstayed her fortnight, and she wouldn't do that.

As they reached the cottage door she asked, 'You're not married, are you?'

'No,' said Paul, 'and nobody's waiting for picture post-cards either.'

She didn't question that, although he was such an attractive man. She felt she had known it, and she poured him a cup of coffee and sat down opposite him to finish her breakfast.

He looked across at the sketchpad and she explained, 'I started some sketches for my wall panel.' If she had stopped to think she might have put that away. You could never be sure how people would react to their own portrait, and Paul's picture didn't flatter him. It was done in exaggerated lines, a near caricature that she could copy in stitching. Pages of sunflowers came first, and the hearts with their cross-stitched message of love. 'Pretty,' commented Paul.

'I'd just started that before I came here. I'm using

yellows and gold. It will be just a little panel, but I think
it might prove a popular line.' Now why had she said
that, when it was planned as a one-off for Douglas? Why
was her voice so cool and professional when it was such
a personal thing?

Paul nodded when he came to the galleons and she
said, 'They have to be simple. They're studies for embroidery. There's a limit to the shading and details you
can get in.'

She wondered if he would recognise himself but he
did, at once, and grinned. 'There's a nose with character,'
he said.

'I shall give him a helmet to balance the nose.'

'You will?' He held the pad at arm's length. 'You
know, I never thought about wearing a helmet. How
much will this wall panel fetch when you've finished it?'

'Depends on how long it takes me.' She pushed aside
her plate and picked up her coffee cup. 'It could work
out about a hundred and fifty a square metre.'

He looked impressed, but he didn't offer to buy it,
which didn't surprise her. She doubted if he had more
than a few pounds to his name. Then he turned the page
and looked at Douglas.

This was a more subtle study. Anna was drawing a
face here, not planning to copy it in other materials, and
Paul asked softly, 'Douglas?'

She disliked the sketch, there was no life in it. She
could have said it wasn't very good, but then they would
have had to talk about Douglas for a little while, and
although she had spoken about him several times she
didn't want to talk about him now. She didn't even want
to say his name.

She nodded and took her plate and mug to the blue
plastic bowl in the sink, and behind her she knew that
Paul had closed her sketching pad.

'Where would you like to go?' he asked, and she
turned, beaming with delight.

'The whole island. We've got the whole island.'

'That's right.'

She decided, 'Let's go and look at the birds today.'

The cliffs where she had first met him were the main nesting area and although most of the birds had taken flight some wintered here. If they climbed the cliffs there would be plenty to see, and when Paul asked, 'Are you a climber?' she smiled.

'I used to be. My grandmother didn't encourage it, but I loved watching the baby birds. Pity it's the wrong time of the year for nesting.'

'The seal cubs are still here.'

'Tomorrow for the seals?' she suggested, and thought how right she had been to come to St Morag's, and how wonderful it was to find this lonely haven.

When they began their walk there was only the sound of the wind across the moorland, and the cries of the birds and their own voices. All this space, filled with clean keen air, was intoxicating, and Anna spread her arms and ran over the heather like a child, or a dancer. Paul ran with her. They leaped small crevices, stunted shrubs, catching hands one moment and loosing them the next, and she laughed, 'I haven't run wild since I was fifteen. If you try it in towns you bump into people.'

'There's only me to bump into here.' He caught her wrist and turned her against him, and her heart came up into her throat and it seemed that all sound ceased as his closeness blotted out everything.

She began to chatter, 'It was warm in the summer, but it hasn't changed up here.' She took another step and they began walking again and she asked him, 'Do you know the songs?'

'What songs?'

'The songs of the islands ... *Westering Home* ... *Charlie is My Darling*. You know.'

Paul grinned, 'I know, but I can't sing them.'

Her grandmother had known them all, they had made

their own entertainment here in the old days, and Anna began to sing as they walked along. She had a strong pure voice and Paul smiled, listening to her, and she was surprised how clearly she was remembering words and tunes. Not only the popular numbers but the old Gaelic songs.

He began to join in with the well-known words and then they sang together. But he listened to the old songs, and they came to the cliffs where the birds nested, Anna crooning a haunting sea song that had surfaced from her subconscious so that it seemed to be singing itself.

They passed the ruins of the cottage and walked along the stony beach to where the cliffs towered above them. As a child she had had her own route up the cliff face, which had differed slightly from one year to the next. But six years had changed the nooks and crannies of weathered sandstone out of all recognition, and she needed Paul's help.

He was taking her up as easily as possible, moving slowly, showing her the jutting pieces that he had tested and found safe, to grip and haul herself up, telling her where to put her feet.

When she had shouted from down below he had been on a ledge about half way up. They were making for that ledge, but almost as soon as Anna began to climb her limbs began to ache. She had walked for miles since she came to the island, with nothing more than a healthy tiredness at the end of the day. But this was infinitely more strenuous than anything she had attempted since her accident, and within a few minutes her right arm was throbbing so badly that she knew she couldn't reach the ledge.

She should never have tried climbing. She should have remembered that arm had been cut nearly to the bone. It might have healed, but it was still an injured limb, not up to swinging on, and she pressed herself against the rock face, feeling the perspiration of pain breaking out on her brow.

'All right?' she heard Paul ask.

'I can't go any further.'

'All right,' he said again, and now his voice was reassuring and calm. 'Take it easy for a minute and we'll go down.'

She closed her eyes and the throbbing seemed to be reaching the scar of every cut and the nerve of each bruise. She had imagined that she was as strong as ever, but after this she would have to accept that her body still had its limits of endurance.

'Shall we go?' said Paul, and reached to grab her arm and that hurt so that she howled:

'Don't touch me!'

'What the hell——' he gasped.

'Sorry, but I was in a car smash before I came here, I got shaken up and that arm has started hurting again. I thought it was O.K. till I tried this.'

'Gently does it,' he said. 'But if you slip I'll have to catch you.'

It was pretty bad getting down. Anna was shaking and aching when she reached the beach and she huddled on the shingle, close to tears. Paul sat down beside her. His eyes seemed very steady. He held her hand and she shook, but he was quiet and still. 'Why didn't you say?' he demanded. 'Why did you let me take you up there?'

'I thought I'd be all right. Well, it was nearly two months ago.' She drew a harsh breath. 'And I'm trying to forget it. I'm trying to pretend it didn't happen.'

He said no more until she had stopped shaking, then he said, 'Let's go home.'

She would be fine again tomorrow, but she had better take it easy for what was left of today. She got up, her legs not quite as steady as she would have wished, and took Paul's arm, leaning on him until they were back on the heathland. Then he turned towards Spanish Sands and she said, 'I want to go to my cottage.'

'I can give you a fish dinner and then you can rest for a while.'

Spanish Sands was nearer than the harbour, and she was feeling shaken. 'Did you catch the fish?' she asked.

'Of course.'

'My, aren't you handy?'

'Aren't I just?'

They were less exuberant walking away than they had been coming here, although she didn't think she had done herself any real damage. At one stage she had been terrified that she might have torn a scar or two, but the throbbing had subsided by the time they reached Spanish Sands.

When they went into Paul's kitchen he said, 'Sit down while I fix a bed for you.'

'I'll be all right just sitting.' She lowered herself into a wooden armchair and grinned, 'I don't need putting to bed, I'm over my convalescence—I'm just not up to climbing cliffs.'

Paul stood, arms crossed, unsmiling, and asked, 'Why did he let you come here on your own?'

'Because he couldn't get away. He has a business to run and a lot of folk depend on him.'

'Do you?'

'Yes, of course,' and she *could* depend on Douglas. She had been overtired and overstressed when she'd doubted him. She said, 'I thought there'd be people here and I could have a couple of quiet weeks' holiday—and I don't particularly want to discuss my fiancé.'

'Then we won't discuss him,' he said cheerfully. He went out of the room and she heard him going up the stairs. He was soon back and he didn't say whether he had fixed a bed for her or not.

The fish was bass, baked in the oven in an earthenware

pot. As he dished up Anna asked, 'How did you catch these?'

'With a rod and line off McNab's Point.'

The fishing boats had been going out when she came here to stay with her grandmother, now Paul took out his little boat and kept his larder stocked. She envied him his self-sufficiency, and wished she had the skills and resources to stay here all winter long.

The fish was good, the best she had tasted in ages, and they had a bottle of red wine that Paul produced. 'With the compliments of the house,' he said. 'I was keeping it for Christmas.'

She wasn't sure if he was joking or not, but her appetite had certainly improved since she came here and as she tucked in she wondered, 'What would have happened to me if I hadn't met you? I'd have wolfed my stock of food in a day or two.'

'You'd have lit your beacon,' he said.

'That wouldn't have been too easy. It's hardly good burning weather. No, I think I'd have broken into one of the high-up houses like this one and sat at an upstairs window flashing S.O.S. with a torch or a lamp.'

'Good idea,' he said approvingly.

'Only I don't know how many dots and dashes make S.O.S.'

'Three dots, three dashes, three dots.'

'I'll remember that.'

They talked about her work. Paul asked her what she liked doing best and she said, 'I enjoy the variety. I might specialise some time, but right now I enjoy it all.' She almost told him about her exhibition, but that seemed like boasting. 'I just love sewing,' she said. 'I'll even darn that tear in your jacket for you if you've got a needle around.'

He looked at his elbow as though it was the first time he had noticed the jagged rip. 'I haven't,' he said regretfully.

'I have, back at the cottage. I could embroider it if you liked. Something long and wavy. Do you fancy a snake?'

'Not much.'

She laughed. 'Please yourself. Invisible darning, then.'

It was a superb meal. Anna enjoyed everything about it, although afterwards she found it hard to keep her eyes open, and when Paul suggested she should rest she said, 'Oh yes, please!'

The wine had made her drowsy, and the climb had exhausted her. Before she started trudging back to the harbour perhaps she should lie down for a while. She looked at her watch, working out the time she must leave to get home well before dark, and Paul said, 'I'll call you in an hour.'

'All right, then.'

'Upstairs and straight ahead.'

There were four closed doors off the dark narrow landing. Anna went to the end, the lino feeling cold to her stockinged feet. The room was cold too, with a big Victorian wardrobe and a chest of drawers filling one wall; and beside the window a dressing table with bulbous legs and a swinging mirror mottled with age, so that when she looked at her reflection she seemed to be peering through a petrified snowstorm.

But there was a duvet on the bed, so this house made some concessions to paying guests, and of course the old-fashioned furniture was part of the attraction. Nobody choosing to holiday on St Morag's wanted to find Habitat in these old houses.

Anna got under the duvet fully dressed and when she lay quietly, without Paul's banter or the stimulus of his company, the little aches began creeping back. She rolled up her sweater sleeve from her tender right arm, and the scars were sore when she touched them. She must have been off her head to think she could pull herself up a steep cliff face. She could walk, she could run, and after a few more months she could probably climb up a cliff face, in time for the nesting season maybe, but not for the rest of this holiday.

She was tired now. She burrowed her head into the comfort of the pillow and pulled the soft duvet up and around her, and was asleep almost at once.

It was dark when she woke. She stirred in her warm little nest and blinked at the blackness through the window and thought—oh good, that settles it, I'll have to stay the night now.

She didn't want to get up. The last thing she wanted was to turn out and walk for miles, and end up in her lonely cottage with nobody there, and the empty harbour and the empty houses. She was cosy. She could hear the wind and the sea and the creaking of the house like footsteps on the stairs. But it didn't matter if there were footsteps here because it would be Paul, not something nameless and scarey.

She wondered how long it would be before he would come up, and her breath quickened and her blood, and a wave of yearning swept over her, as urgent as though his lips kissed her breasts, and he was lying here beside her.

She struggled to sit up, throwing the duvet aside, the warm cocoon of dreams shattered, because she hadn't come to St Morag's to let this happen. It wasn't her fault that she had met a man here whom she fancied, wanted, but casual affairs had never been for her. She was wearing Douglas's ring and the loyalty that was an integral part of her nature was revolted by the weakness that had had her eager for Paul's lovemaking, even if she was half asleep.

It shocked her awake. She sat up, hating herself, lying here waiting to welcome a near-stranger into her bed. But by the time she had swung her feet on to the floor she had turned most of the anger and all the blame on to Paul.

He had promised to wake her. He knew why she was set against staying the night. He had given her wine with her meal, and he knew she was shaken up and that once she fell asleep she might sleep heavily until it was dark, and he had *promised*. And she had been a fool to believe him.

She felt her way along the landing and down the stairs until the light from the kitchen reached her. The door was open, and the light was a lamp on the kitchen table at which Paul was sitting, writing on lined foolscap paper with a ballpoint pen.

Anna took in all the scene, even to wondering exactly what he was writing, although she was blazing with indignation. He hadn't heard her coming and he didn't look up until she demanded, 'Writing your play?'

Then he looked, and after a moment he said, 'Yes.'

'Sorry to disturb you,' she said tartly. 'Hadn't you noticed that it was getting dark?'

Of course he'd noticed. He'd lit the lamp. Outside the night was pitch black. 'Be a good child,' he said, 'and make some coffee.'

He thought she'd accept that she was stuck here now, and that wasn't hospitality. 'All right,' she said. 'But then I'm going home.'

'Don't be stupid.' He still had the pen on the paper. If she had stayed she wondered if he would have read her his play, and whether it was any good, and what he had planned for afterwards. No, she didn't wonder about that. She knew what he had planned.

'I am not staying here,' she said.

'Why not?' Paul put down the pen then and waited as though he expected an answer. But he was as aware as she of the sexual attraction between them. He knew exactly what a night together could mean, she didn't have to spell it out for him, and her lips set.

'Are you scared I'll try to make love to you?' His dark eyes gleamed with bright mockery. 'Or scared that you'll let me?'

He knew what could happen and he was confident that it would, but he didn't know her. 'I don't play around,' said Anna. She was twisting her ring until she saw him watching her restless fingers, then she locked them together so that it looked as though she was praying for something. Mercy, perhaps. Or just to get out of here.

'I believe you,' he said. 'Don't you trust me?'

'No.'

'Shrewd girl.' He came towards her, where she stood in the doorway, and she needed all her anger because she didn't want to walk those dark miles home, but she was going right now.

She went past him to get her boots, from where she had left them by the stove, so angry that if he had touched her she would have lashed out. She nearly over-balanced, standing on one leg to pull on the second boot, and staggered wildly for a moment before she hopped to a chair.

Neither spoke. Nor while Anna was fastening up her oilskins and pushing her hair into a woolly cap. Paul watched every move, and she suspected that if she had looked directly at him he would have burst out laughing.

He thought she'd lost her temper. He didn't think she'd go—or if she did he expected her to turn back before she lost sight of this house.

'Could I trouble you for a torch?' she asked with icy politeness.

'No trouble.' He opened a drawer and produced a hefty black-rubber covered torch, with a beam like a search-light. It was heavy as a truncheon, but she wasn't likely to be attacked on the way. She might fall over a sheep or down a hole, but the winter crime rate was nil on St Morag's.

'Goodnight,' she said, as she opened the back door and the night wind came in like a scythe.

'Goodnight,' he said. 'You can always come back.'

'Don't bank on that,' and she switched on the torch which lightened the blackness into a weird grey of unfamiliar shapes and shadows. Then she marched doggedly away from the house, looking back after a few minutes. She had thought Paul might follow her, but the door hadn't opened and she was on her own.

Well, she wasn't returning. It wasn't raining. It was cold and the mist, rising from the sea, was filling the hollows and clinging wispily to ruined buildings and misshapen shrubs. But the broken road ran straight. If she kept to it she would end up down in the harbour, in her own cottage; and after this she never wanted to set eyes on Paul Peralta again.

She kept going, as fast as she dared, at a jog trot, but tonight the island seemed haunted by the vanished people who had lived here. As the mist moved and the wind howled her imagination ran riot, until she could see drifting figures crossing her path, and hear soft footsteps following. She turned her torch back down the road and the emptiness of that made her teeth chatter.

There were no other lights but her torch now. The lamplight from the kitchen where she had left Paul was far behind her, and it was a night without moon or stars. If she could have whistled in the dark she might have done, to keep up her spirits. She tried to sing, although she was getting breathless, but the wind turned the melody into eerie echoes that were more unnerving than silence.

After that she used her breath for running and, considering how dark it was, she must have covered the distance in record time. She was coming down the hill to the harbour fast enough to have gone over the broken wall into the water, if she hadn't pulled herself together and slowed down, just before she reached the gulley.

But she still ran, and dashed into her cottage as though something would have got her if she had hung around outside. The door wasn't locked. Nobody was likely to break in while she was out, but she turned the key now and shot the bolt, then put the torch on the table and lit the lamp by its light.

That headlong flight hadn't been very clever. She should have walked, because there was nothing that could have hurt her on St Morag's, except the roughness of the ground that might have sent her sprawling any time. She was still breathing hard, even after she had sat slumped at the table for several minutes.

All she could face tonight was bed again. If Paul had called her while it was still daylight, and she had come back quietly, she would have been all right, but now she felt like nothing on earth. She made up the fire with peat, undressed and crawled into her sleeping bag, aching from head to foot.

For the first time she took a sleeping pill, but even so the old bruises ached again and for the first time she was conscious that the sofa was hard. Tomorrow she'd go upstairs and see what the mattresses were like up there. Damp probably, but probably more comfortable than this.

She had to make a real effort to put aside her resentment against Paul. That nightmare dash across the island had been all his fault. But so long as she let her mind go on churning the sleeping drug wouldn't work.

Forget it, she ordered herself. Forget him. Go to sleep now. She moved carefully, trying to find a more comfortable position, promising herself that tomorrow she would be fighting fit again, and then she would tell Paul Peralta a thing or two.

But next morning she woke in a calmer frame of mind. The mist was still hanging around and the deserted harbour still looked eerie, but of course by daylight fog was fog and nothing else, and her panic flight of the night before seemed ridiculous. She wouldn't be telling anybody about that. Nor that she had half believed that ghosts were after her.

She had stopped aching. She dressed and prepared her breakfast, and now she was beginning to admit to herself that she had made an unnecessary fuss. Not in coming back here for the night—that was sensible—but in carrying on as though Paul was an old-time melodrama seducer.

This morning she could see his point of view. He couldn't understand why they shouldn't share a house, instead of living at opposite ends of the island, nor why they shouldn't sleep together if they wanted to.

He wanted her and he thought she wanted him; and she did, but she had principles that she had no intention of chucking to the winds. Paul was for taking all they could get from the days and nights they were alone together on St Morag's. Then, when she wanted to leave, he would sail her back to Carra and they would say goodbye, and perhaps, 'See you again some time.' Anna would go back to Douglas and there would be no hard feelings. 'I had a nice holiday,' she would tell her friends. 'I had fun.'

But that wasn't how she lived her life, although it would be all too easy to go a little mad here, to answer the call of the wild that Paul stirred in her blood; and that was good enough reason for cutting short her stay on St Morag's.

She would tell him she wanted to leave now. As soon as she saw him she would ask him to get his boat out and put her down, either on the mainland or on one of the bigger islands where she could find lodgings for the rest of her two weeks. She wasn't ready to return home yet, but St Morag's was a bleak and bitter place these days. She would be safer away from here, and away from Paul.

She didn't go looking for him, but she was pretty certain that he would be along quite soon. After all, he had let her walk off alone into the darkness, and she expected him to come down to the harbour this morning to reassure himself she had arrived safely.

But he didn't. He didn't come all day. So either he was annoyed and waiting for her to go back and make the peace—in which case he'd wait a long time. Or he wasn't bothering, and he'd come calling when it suited him.

Either was off-putting and uncomplimentary, and if it hadn't been for the boat she would have taken steps to avoid him from now on. Anna didn't go far herself that day. She worked on the wall panel designs and during the afternoon she walked around the harbour, and then up the hill.

At the top of the hill she looked all ways to see if there was any sign of Paul, but the mist made visibility patchy and she didn't go any further. She came down the hill again and settled into the cottage for a cosy early night.

They should have gone looking for seals today. Tomorrow she would go herself, and if Paul wasn't at the cove she would go to his house. She couldn't stay here alone much longer. The weather was so erratic that she should be taking her first opportunity to get away. They'd already had a thunderstorm and now the fog was starting to close in. She could be stuck if she didn't watch out. So tomorrow she would have to look Paul up again, and ask him about his boat.

Tomorrow he came. She had taken another sleeping pill and slept late, and she was outside, wearing a coat over her pyjamas and opening the shutters, when he came round the corner from the gulley and called, 'Hi!'

'Oh, it's you.' She went back inside, grabbing her clothes and running upstairs with them. In the first bedroom she slipped off her coat and wriggled out of her pyjamas, dragging on jumper and jeans. The zip stuck on her jeans and Paul shouted from downstairs, 'Where are you?'

'Coming!' She jerked frantically, forcing the zip up with material caught between the teeth.

'How nice of you to call,' she said crisply, and heard him laugh.

'I'm like that.'

She didn't really like him. He was a shiftless drifter compared to Douglas, but almost any company was better than none, and she had been bored yesterday. She wasn't sorry he was here.

He was putting on the kettle when she came down the stairs. 'I got back safely, thank you,' Anna said coolly.

'Of course you did,' he said. 'A strong determined girl like you.' He looked across at the sleeping bag on the sofa. 'Did you enjoy your lonely couch?'

'Oh, shut up!' she snapped. It was too early for repartee, and she picked up her comb and began to drag it through her hair, wincing at a tangle, demanding, 'If I stay here are you going to go on making idiotic passes?'

Paul fetched himself a cup from the kitchen cupboard and put it down on the table beside her cup and saucer. He was making a pass now, laying himself a place at her table, and she turned away because he was going to grin and this was not funny.

'You can save yourself the trouble,' she said. 'I'm not interested. I'm an oddity, a one-man woman.' She put down the comb and went into the kitchen to wait for the kettle to boil, and heard Paul pull up another chair to the table.

'He should have come with you,' he said.

'I wouldn't have let him.'

'Why not?'

'Because I wanted to come here alone,' and she came to the kitchen door to face him. 'But I didn't know I was going to be alone when I got here, did I? I didn't know the island was going to be deserted and this is a pretty peculiar situation, just you and me. Folk could get the wrong idea. You *have* got the wrong idea, so I would appreciate it if you would get out your boat and get me off here.'

'But you haven't seen the seals.' He sounded as though she was about to leave without visiting old friends, who would be saddened by her neglect. 'Come and see the seals and I'll take you back tomorrow,' he coaxed, and she had difficulty holding back a smile. A day couldn't make much difference. She would like to see the seals.

She said, 'Is that a promise, about tomorrow?'

'Of course.'

She tried to look severe, reminding him, 'But you don't keep promises.'

'Usually.' His smile was infectious. Against her will it made her lips twitch and she couldn't keep on frowning. 'This time I will,' he said.

Anna wanted to leave, of course, but there was no mad rush, tomorrow would do. 'All right,' she said. 'Tomorrow.'

While she had breakfast he looked at the designs she had made yesterday, and then they walked towards the cove and the caves where the seals gathered. She was taking it easier today, no jumping over crevices or clambering up cliffs; but she felt as fit as ever, and much happier than she had done yesterday, all alone.

The sands were firm and almost pure white, with a gentle slope down to the water. Where they curved back into the cliff face there were deep caves that the sea had excavated over the centuries and which at high tide or storm wrack boomed with the inrush of water.

Out in the sea was a double chain of rocks, some quite tall, others washed over by breakers, and on and around the rocks the seals were playing, sliding happily down the grey-black rock into the waves, curving like dolphins over the crests, vanishing and reappearing.

Cub seals, dwarfed by their parents, were kept in check by a flick of a flipper or the beat of a tail in the water; and Anna and Paul sat protected by a windbreak of rock and it was all a delight.

She wished she had a camera; she had never seen the cub seals before. She huddled in her thick jumper and oilskins and boots and forgot discomfort. She said, 'They're beautiful. They don't cull them here, do they?'

'This is a sanctuary,' said Paul, and it was. It felt like the safest place in the world.

They watched the tide come in, leaving a narrow edge of sand with most of the caves in the bay under water, and Anna could have stayed all day. She would be leaving the island tomorrow, this was her first and last chance to come down here, and she was willing to stay until the last possible moment.

Paul seemed content enough, sitting there. They didn't do much talking, but there was a feeling of companionship between them that didn't need words. He would touch her arm and point, and her gaze would follow and she would smile. It seemed that the seals played for them, putting on a display. 'Do you come here often?' she asked.

'Yes,' he said, 'and so should you.'

Anna wished she had. Every so often a black round head would emerge from the water, whiskered, and watching them with solemn round eyes before disappearing. She was regretting that as a child she had never visited her grandmother in the winter. The long vacation, the summer holidays, had always been her visiting time. Since her grandmother's death the years had passed, but after this she would come again.

Did Paul only come in the winter? she wondered. When the lodgings were free. Next Easter she would be married, and it wouldn't matter to her when Paul came to the island. She supposed she would be married, and Douglas would hate this place when there was fog and bitter cold winds and all the houses were empty.

If he had been with her now, watching the seals, he would have been shivering and asking if she was ready to go back to the fire ages ago. He wouldn't have come down the beach. He wouldn't have come to the island. She caught herself thinking of Douglas with amusement, and a little pity, as detached as though he was no more than an acquaintance.

The fog was still about, not thick, more of a mist, but enough to prevent them seeing right out to sea, and they didn't hear the dinghy. The first warning of intruders was the sound of splashing oars, and voices.

They heard that together and turned to look at each other. 'We've got visitors,' said Paul, and Anna's first reaction was annoyance as though anyone else must be trespassing, because it had been quite perfect, just her and Paul, and the seals and the birds.

But of course other folk had the right to land, and the sightseers might give her a lift off the island. There must be a bigger boat out there, she should be asking if she could leave with them, but she sat still, because she didn't really want to leave yet.

Altogether the mood of blissful content was being spoiled and she sighed, watching the approach of the rowing boat between the rocks.

Beside her Paul was silent, and when she began to say, 'I suppose I could ask———' he silenced her with a gesture. A chill ran through her. Something was wrong. They were almost hidden by their screen of overhanging and encircling rock, but Paul's attitude was wary and watchful. He leaned forward a little, eyes narrowed in a face that was suddenly grim, then he put out a hand, his arm across Anna holding her back as she tried to question him without speaking.

But he wasn't looking at her, so her expression of query and alarm was wasted. He was watching the dinghy and the three men aboard it as an anchor went over the side, and the men clambered out on to the rocks near the caves.

One man carried a gun, the other two clubs, and Anna gasped, 'I thought you said the seals were safe here?'

As she spoke the sound of shots rang out and echoed as the man fired into a cave, followed by a great splashing of seals, coming through the narrow entrance, swimming for what they believed was the safety of the open sea.

The men were keeping back from the cave entrance, but the one who had fired had his gun raised shoulder-high and Anna screamed 'No!' and slithered beneath Paul's arm, down on to the sand, starting to run towards the ledge of rock edging the caves.

'What the hell do you think you're doing?' Paul shouted, with such authority in his voice that Anna stopped dead, on her foothold of rock, and one of the men yelled:

'Who the blazes are you?'

'I'm a coastguard!' Paul roared. 'And this is protected area, as you bloody well know, so get your stinking selves away from here!'

That man had the gun, the other two had clubs that could have battered in a human skull as easily as a seal's. But perhaps they thought that where there was one coastguard there would be others. Perhaps they were out for the easy money of a few seals' skins but not prepared to fight for them. They were three against one unarmed man and a girl, but Paul's dark figure on the beach carried such menace and controlled violence that Anna was not at all surprised to see them drawing back. He scared her, and she was on his side.

One by one they scrambled back into the dinghy, yanking up the anchor, and the oars dipped and rose so fast that it was almost a panic rout. The boat was through the rocks and vanishing into the mist while she was still staring and gasping, and suddenly, out of the cave into which the shots had been fired, came the biggest seal they had seen today.

A monster seal, roaring with anger. Anna leapt back in terror, slipping into the water which was about waist-deep beneath the shelf of rock on which she was standing, so that she ran splashing out of the freezing cold waves and Paul came running towards her, and the bull seal was nearly on them.

Paul grabbed her arm and ran with her towards the path up from the cove. When she stumbled he dragged her until she regained her balance. She could hear the bellowing beast behind them, but she didn't stop to look round until they were high up from the cove, and she wouldn't have stopped then if Paul hadn't said, 'We're all right now.'

Then she looked down at the vast shape below, still roaring defiance, whiskers bristling, snarling mouth and wrinkling snout. There were patches on its hide from other bloody combats, and it was the most terrifying sight she had ever seen.

'What's that?' she croaked.

'Big Daddy,' said Paul. 'He'd have had that boat over if we'd left him to it. Perhaps we should have done. A pity he can't tell friends from enemies.'

'He'd have killed us, wouldn't he? He'd have gone over us like a tank if he could have caught us.' He was massive as a tank, and still snarling.

'Only in protection of the herd,' said Paul.

'Good for him! Only he can't tell friends from

enemies.' Her sodden boots and dragging oilskins were suddenly weighing like lead, although she had hardly been aware of them in her dash out of the water and along the beach, with Big Daddy snorting in her wake.

'Let's get away from here,' she begged. 'That was horrible! You know, when I heard that boat coming I was all set to ask if I could hitch a lift.'

She took a step, and screeched as pain shot through her ankle. Something else she had been too distraught to notice. When she'd stumbled down there she had turned her foot, but she had gone right on running until she was safe up here.

'Oh, my gosh,' she muttered. 'That's all I need!'

She was shivering as though she had ague, and Paul held her close for a moment. Then he lifted her in his arms, as though she was no weight at all. 'Come on, my bonny bird,' he said, 'you can't fly away now.'

He was smiling, making her smile, but as she looked up into the hawkish face above her she knew that it was true and that there was no escape.

CHAPTER FIVE

'TAKE off your oilskins and put this on.' Paul replaced Anna gently on her feet and undid his Windbreaker, and she started to protest. But her teeth were chattering so that she only got out:

'Really I can't,' before he had her out of her oilskins and into his jacket. That was dry and thick, but underneath it she was wet to the skin and she had never been so cold in her life.

Then he picked her up again, and she hadn't realised how strong he was. He carried her all the way from the caves of the seals to Spanish Sands without once stopping to rest. It wasn't so much the distance as the roughness of the ground that should have been the problem, and she was astounded that he never needed to put her down, because she was a tallish girl. But he carried her as if she was a child in his arms and she realised that the lean hard body must be tough as tempered steel.

She was so glad to see the fire burning in the kitchen range when they reached the house where Paul was living, and she took off the Windbreaker and crooned with pleasure as the heat reached her hands and face. Paul stirred the peat and she crouched as close as she dared, from where he had put her, on the rug in front of the fire. Although the heat seemed to stay on the surface of her skin, her bones could have been packed in ice.

She sat on the floor and began to pull off a boot and he took hold of her foot and yanked while she held on to the table leg.

'They'll take some drying,' she said as the boot came off. The clammy leather felt repulsive, and when she lifted her other foot she moaned. In the boot her ankle had swollen and when she prodded it gingerly it was excruciating. The prospect of dragging off the boot petrified her.

'I can't shift it,' she muttered. 'It's swollen. No,' as he squatted down beside her, 'don't yank it. I think it's broken.'

'Can't be.' He reminded her, 'You ran up the hill on it,' and she snorted :

'With Big Daddy behind me I'd have run if it had fallen off!' He moved to touch and she said sharply, 'Leave it alone!' She glared at him until he dropped his hand and stood up. 'I'll sit with it up,' she announced, 'and when the swelling's gone down I should be able to get the boot off. What do you think you're going to do with that?'

Paul was taking a carving knife out of a drawer in the dresser. 'Cut the boot,' he said.

'No!' She had only one pair of decent boots with her and she didn't want them ruined. She wished she had worn her wellingtons today.

'You can't get your pants off if you're wearing a boot,' he said reasonably, and Anna knew that she couldn't sit around in soaking wet jeans and tights. Unless he was proposing ripping those off her too. She said crossly :

'They're my best boots. They cost the earth.'

'You shouldn't have gone swimming in them.'

'It wasn't the water that made my ankle swell.' Although the salt water had probably ruined the leather. She sighed, 'Very well then. Is that knife sharp?' She didn't want her foot jolted around while he sawed away at her boot, and he pantomimed testing the edge on his thumb.

'The sharpest in the house. Do you need a bullet to bite on?'

He could joke. It wasn't his ankle—nor his boot. She

said tartly, 'You're not proposing to cut my leg off?'

'Only as a last resort.' He grinned like Sweeney Todd and she joked, 'The mad doctor strikes again.'

'I'll cut the seam.' He knelt beside her, nicking the stitching down the front of her boot very carefully; but her ankle was throbbing away and her wet clothes were sticking to her. She sneezed explosively and he said, 'Bless you.'

'Thanks, I could use a blessing.' She looked at the thick black hair on his bowed head and thought she would like to twine her fingers in it. She needed to hold on to something, she was feeling lousier by the minute. Her bones were still frozen and yet she could have sworn she was starting to run a temperature.

He put down the knife and ripped the seam and she gasped, 'Ouch!'

'All right?' He looked up quite anxiously, and she could feel tears in her eyes.

'My beautiful Spanish boots,' she said, but the tears were because she was feeling so ill. She pressed her clasped hands to her mouth and he eased her foot out of her boot. It was very swollen. Her jeans were tight around it like a denim blue sausage.

'I'll get you something to wear,' he said. 'Get out of those!'

She took her soaking wet sweater and vest over her head. Her bra was wet through too, but that could wait until she had some covering. That darn zip wouldn't budge, and she picked up the carving knife which he'd left on the floor to try to snip it free.

As Paul came back into the room, carrying clothes, the firelight glinted on the knife and he said, 'Hara-kiri or self-defence?'

'I've got some material in my zip.' She could cut herself twisting round to hack away with the long sharp knife. She asked, 'Do you have any scissors?'

'These any good?'

They were kitchen scissors, but easier to manipulate than the carving knife, and Anna took them from him. Her scars felt livid and angry. Paul saw them, of course, but he showed no reaction. As soon as he'd handed her the scissors he proceeded to display the clothes he'd brought downstairs: a shirt, a sweater, some fisherman's socks and a pair of Y-fronts.

He held them up gravely, one by one, as though she was selecting from a model collection, then put them on a chair in a pile, and at the Y-fronts she burst out laughing. 'I shan't need self-defence in those!'

He looked surprised, as though the customer had criticised the goods. 'I'm sure madam will find they make her look extremely seductive.'

'They may work for you,' she grinned, and he said:

'Well, thank you, madam. We aim to please.'

When she stopped grinning she had to clench her jaws to stop her teeth starting to chatter again. Hot and cold. Freezing and burning. She'd caught a chill, falling into the sea, that was what she'd done, and she had to get out of these wet things. But when she twisted round to try to free the zip, her eyes stung and her head pounded and she straightened up gasping.

'Damn the thing!' She sounded petulant, she felt so weak, so stupid. 'Yank this for me, will you?'

'Sure.' His fingers brushing against her were strangely soothing. She wished he would draw her close and go on stroking her, because she needed to be warmed and comforted. When he had coaxed the zip apart he eased jeans and tights over the swollen ankle. He was undressing her, quietly, gently, as though she was a tired child. When he undid her bra she knew she was ill because she couldn't be bothered to raise her hands and slip the straps from her shoulders. She was just thankful that somebody was doing it for her, without sexuality or fuss.

She sneezed again as the shirt went over her head, and again against the tickling wool of the sweater, and sat huddled with the warmth of the fire on her face as Paul went out of the room. He brought back one of the small armchairs from the parlour, then a second trip to fetch a duvet, and by drawing up a kitchen chair there was a makeshift sofa for her.

When she was seated in the armchair and wrapped in the duvet he bandaged her ankle, and she waited for him to say something. There was nothing she could think of to say, except 'Thank you' or 'Aren't you the handy one?' But somehow she couldn't break the silence.

Paul looked up, from tucking in the ends of the bandage around her ankle, and said, 'It was a bad smash.' She nodded and he smiled, 'They'll fade. You're very beautiful.'

She hadn't felt any embarrassment while he was getting her out of her wet clothing, her nakedness had seemed like that of a patient and doctor, but when he said she was beautiful she blushed hotly and began to chatter to hide her blush.

'I was lucky,' she said. 'I skidded into a lamp-post in the rain and the car was a write-off, but all I got were cuts and bruises. The cuts were messy, but in the end there won't be much to show. Only now I've done it again.' She grimaced at her ankle. 'I hope accidents don't run in threes. I came here for a quiet holiday somewhere safe and peaceful. But, like it did for the seals, today, it's turned out to be a pretty savage sanctuary.'

'You need a sanctuary?' asked Paul quietly, and she told him again:

'I needed a quiet holiday. Do you often get illegal seal hunters?'

'The bull seal certainly knew what the sound of rifle shots meant.' He started opening a tin of soup, and she wondered:

'If we go down there again will he be waiting for us?'

'Not unless we go in with guns and clubs.' He poured the soup into the saucepan, stirred it a couple of times, and said, 'But we won't, will we? Because you're leaving tomorrow.'

Only if she made a miracle recovery overnight. She couldn't travel anywhere in this state, but as soon as she could travel she wanted to go. She nestled deeper in her duvet and Paul said, 'You do want to go tomorrow?'

'Yes, I do. They aren't expecting me home until a week on Sunday——'

'Douglas isn't expecting you home?' he interrupted.

'That's what I said. So I'm going to find a small hotel for the rest of the time. St Morag's is turning out to be too rugged for me.'

But that wasn't the whole reason for her leaving in a hurry, that was not a reason at all. She wanted out because the explosive force between them was burning on too short a fuse, and at the end of her two weeks she wasn't going home with her conscience torturing her or, even worse and just as likely, so turned on by Paul that she couldn't bear to leave him.

Paul brought her a mug of soup and as she leaned forward to take it he put a hand on her forehead, and whistled soundlessly. 'Are you getting a temperature?'

'I think I am.'

'There are some aspirins somewhere, and I know there's a hot water bottle. You'd better get to bed.'

Anna smiled wanly, 'Every time I come here you seem to be putting me to bed,' and he grinned back at her.

'If that goes in threes I hope you're in better condition next time.'

She nearly said, 'So do I,' but she wasn't quite that lightheaded.

She took the aspirins, and a cup of hot tea instead of

the soup, then Paul helped her up to bed which was warmed by a stone hot water bottle that would have been murder if she had knocked her foot against it. She was in for a streaming cold, and she would be lucky if she wasn't in for pneumonia. Big Daddy was a health hazard, and she had never been so scared in her life.

Except when she stood in the hall of Douglas's home and heard them saying that she might have gone blind. That had been the greatest terror, and as her temperature rose her sleep filled with nightmares in which she was running from monsters through fog rising like steam, burning and blinding her. She couldn't see. She ran blind and screaming.

She woke burning, the shirt she was wearing drenched in sweat; and she lay listening to her thumping heart-beats and trying to swallow. Her throat was the only dry part of her. Hair and skin were slippery with perspiration, but her throat was full of sand, and if she didn't get a drink right away it was going to silt up and choke her.

She tried to call out, but the only sound she made was a pathetic squeak. A lamp was lit, standing on the ugly old dressing table and reflected in the patchy mirror, and she sat up in bed, scarlet-faced, hair sticking to her forehead and falling in limp strands over her face.

She looked terrible but she felt worse, and if she didn't get a drink she would burn up. She had to get some cold water. Her throat was burning sand, her tongue was filling her mouth. It took all her strength to lift the duvet and she rolled out of bed. But when she tried to stand her ankle gave way and she fell full length with a mighty crash. She had forgotten her ankle. She screamed in agony and Paul came rushing into the room.

The scream had burst out of her, but when she tried to speak her throat closed up again and she could only make faint whispery sounds. He picked her up and put her back on the bed and she croaked, 'I want a drink.'

'All right.' She was more than a little delirious because everything was swimming around her, the lamp, the room, Paul's dark face. She lay back, but he seemed to be back almost before her eyes closed, putting an arm around her and a cup to her lips.

The drink was hot and her throat hurt when she tried to gulp it down. She croaked, 'I want some cold water.'

'Drink this,' said Paul, and because she was thirsty, and because she was too weak to do anything except what she was told, Anna drank it. And swallowed the aspirins.

'Don't go,' she gasped. 'Stay with me.'

'Of course I'll stay.'

'I'm having nightmares about bull seals.' He sat on the bed and smoothed her hair back from her hot forehead and she looked at him with swimming smarting eyes, and reached to hold his hand 'Don't let it catch me,' she said. 'And get under the cover, you'll catch your death of cold.'

She slept again after that. When she lifted her heavy head it was morning and the lamp was out. She turned to look for Paul, she had held on to his hand until she fell asleep. He wasn't here now, although she knew he would come back soon and she didn't feel alone.

But she did feel very fragile and her ankle jabbed when she tried to move it. She wasn't leaving St Morag's today, that was for sure, and from what she could see the fog was opaque against the windows, so Paul would have every excuse for not taking his boat out.

A fine rest this holiday had turned out to be! She had come to recuperate physically and look at the shape she was in; and to do some calm thinking about Douglas, and most of the time Douglas had been the last thing on her mind.

She really must start thinking about Douglas, but just then Paul walked in, dressed in black sweater and pants.

Last night she had a vague memory of falling asleep with her head on his bare chest. She wondered if she had got him out of bed when she fell and screamed. She announced in a cracked voice, 'I've decided to live.'

'And why not?' Paul sounded entirely approving.

'If I can just get through the next twenty-four hours.' She sniffed and winced. 'My head feels as if it's stuffed with hot pepper!' Eyes and nose were stinging, and her head was aching. She asked, 'What was in that drink you gave me?'

'Whisky.' She hadn't realised that. It had scalded her throat all the way down, but she had been too woozy to worry, or wonder what it was. She said, 'So this *is* a hangover.'

She remembered her headaches after her accident, but this wasn't like that. This was because she had caught a kingsize chill and been dosed with an outsize whisky. But she put her hand in front of her eyes and shivered a little. Then she said, 'Sorry to be such a nuisance, I was having nightmares last night. Monster seals were chasing me.' She licked her dry lips and tried to smile. 'I couldn't see,' she said. Paul was looking at her very hard, and she wondered if she might have babbled in her feverish sleep, while he was lying beside her.

She said, 'I don't remember much after the whisky, except dragging you into bed,' and was glad when he grinned because if she had talked about going blind he surely wouldn't be laughing.

'But only to hold your hand,' he said.

She managed a cackle of laughter herself, and croaked, 'I'm not going far today, am I?'

'Downstairs perhaps, I've lit a fire in the parlour and there's a sofa there. I could bring a heater up here if you'd prefer it, but this is a dreary little room.'

'I'd like to come downstairs.'

'I'll get you a drink.' He stood for a moment smiling at

her, his eyes gypsy dark and bright, and she knew that
if she reached for him now and pulled him down beside
her he wouldn't settle for holding hands.

'No more whisky,' she said.

'You should be so lucky.'

'What is this?' she asked when she'd sipped from the
mug he brought up a few minutes later, and Paul raised
both eyebrows.

'Tea.'

'I've lost my taste.' That was why she hadn't recognised the whisky last night. 'It could be coffee. I can't
smell it either.' But she drank it all and handed back the
mug. The shirt she was wearing was stiff. After the way
she had perspired last night she badly needed a change
of clothing, and she asked, 'Can you lend me another
shirt?'

'You can't go on like this,' he said severely. 'They don't
grow on trees, you know.'

'Got anything in orange?' she asked. 'That's really my
colour.' She plucked at the collar of the white cotton shirt
she was wearing. 'This does nothing for me.'

'But you do plenty for it.' said Paul.

Anna knew how she looked, she could see herself in
the mirror and she looked a wreck. She said, 'What I
would like more than anything in the world is a bath, but
I'll settle for a bowl of water.'

'Here or downstairs?'

She needed to stay in bed, but downstairs she would be
a little less bother. Suppose this had happened to her and
she had been alone, no Paul? Suppose she had been alone
watching the seals when the hunters came? She would
have lost her head, just the same, and screamed out at
them, but they wouldn't have run away from her. And
the bull seal, would the hunters have shot him? Was the
rifle powerful enough to stop an animal that size? If
Paul hadn't had her arm when she stumbled she wouldn't
have got away.

'Hey,' said Paul softly, and she looked up into his face. He was leaning over her and he tapped her cheek very gently. 'Don't go into a brown study over it.'

'What?'

'Upstairs or downstairs?'

'Oh, I'll come down. I was just thinking how awful it would have been if I'd been feeling as rotten as this, and I'd been all by myself on the island.'

He smiled. 'But you wouldn't be by yourself. You called up one of the dark men, so you can never be alone again.'

'Goody,' she said. She would be sorry when they had to part, because she would always remember Paul. Like the island he would always have a place in her heart.

He left her in the parlour, swathed in her duvet on the sofa, and by the time she had got downstairs she was glad to rest again. The fever had raged through her last night, she was washed out now, but her temperature was down. Her plunge into the icy sea was not going to end in pneumonia after all.

This was a room from which there was the wonderful view over Spanish Sands, but not today. Today the window was blanketed in fog. The house was utterly closed in. It looked solid out there, as though you could open the window and find you were facing a white wall which would bounce your voice back at you if you shouted.

It would have been grim in the cottage by the harbour. She wouldn't have dared take a step outside. Two steps and you would be lost. If she had to be shut in thank heaven for her fellow prisoner. All in all this was a cosy little prison.

The door of the parlour was open, and she could hear Paul moving around if she listened. He didn't make much noise, he mostly seemed to go around the house barefoot, but she could hear him, and this morning she was very aware of him again—as a man who wanted to make love to her, and to whom she was dangerously attracted. Last night she had grabbed him and held him, because she was scared to be alone. Last night she was feverish and ill, but she would think twice before she grabbed him again because next time he would surely grab her back. She laughed softly to herself and closed her eyes, and perhaps she slept a little, because next thing she knew Paul was saying, 'This way.'

She blinked. 'This way to what?' There was a chemical toilet in a very small room leading off the hall, but she had called in there on her way from the bedroom. He must mean to the kitchen to wash. 'All right,' she said. She leaned on his shoulder to walk. There were walking sticks in the hallstand and she could use one of those as soon as she was just a little stronger.

In the kitchen doorway she stopped with a gasp. 'Hey!' she exclaimed. 'Luxury! They didn't have one of these in my cottage.'

'This is two-star service up here,' said Paul. In the middle of the kitchen was a large tin bath, half filled with water from which steam rose.

Anna asked, 'Where did it come from?' and he nodded towards a tall narrow cupboard, explaining:

'You heat up the water in the washing boiler and fill it with buckets.'

It was primitive, but it was better than no bath at all. 'Not exactly the most convenient place to have a bath.' She could see difficulties, like no privacy.

'Of course it is,' said Paul. 'By the fire. You can have your supper—or in this case your breakfast—while you're soaking.'

'Breakfast will have to wait.' She looked up at the pendulum clock ticking away on the wall. 'Can you give me, say, ten minutes?'

'You can manage?'

'Yes, thank you.'

He said ruefully, 'You have made a quick recovery,' and Anna smiled. She hadn't really recovered, her voice was still hoarse, she had lost her sense of taste and smell and she had caught a shocking cold—not to mention spraining her ankle. But she was no longer completely helpless, and from now on she was undressing and dressing herself.

'Out,' she ordered.

'Shout if you need anything.' She couldn't shout, and Paul picked up the boot he had cut off her last night and placed it by the bath. 'On second thoughts,' he said, 'throw this at the door.'

He closed the door after him and she sat down and began to unwrap her bandaged ankle. It was sprained all right, but the swelling had gone down. Like her it was on the road to recovery. Then she got out of the sweater and shirt, and by leaning on the table—lucky the bath was by the side of it—she managed to lower herself into the water.

It was a good big tin bath. You could put the children in it together, or it could accommodate the man of the household. She could imagine mothers kneeling in front of the fire, wearing big cover-all aprons, with two or three squirming squealing high-spirited children larking around in this tub.

That was why the islanders had left, to get nice bright ordinary bathrooms. But water that came hot from the tap wasn't the same as water that meant somebody had filled the copper and lit the fire under it, and carried bucket after bucket to tip into the old tin bath.

This was special service, four star at least. Anna washed quickly, although she would have quite enjoyed lazing in the bath, in front of the fire, until the water cooled around her. But after the ten minutes she had said she needed Paul could be opening the door to ask if all was well.

He had washed her clothes, they hung across the kitchen on a line. Very domestic, she thought, and knew it proved nothing of the sort. What it proved was that he could make a home for himself any time, anywhere. He could always travel in comfort, alone.

Her undies were dry, but her sweater and jeans were still much too damp to wear, so she helped herself to the clean shirt hanging on the back of a chair which she hoped he had put out for her. And a navy blue cardigan. Cashmere. That surprised her. He'd done himself well there, unless it was a present. She wondered what the women in Paul's life were like. She had told him about Douglas, but he hadn't told her about anybody, except that there was no one. No wife, nobody expecting him to drop them a line, and she really couldn't believe that when he was so attractive and so sexy.

The kettle was half full of warm water and she hopped over to the sink and lathered her hair with the bar of white unscented soap she had just used in her bath. The water from the hand pump over the sink was rainwater, of course, soft as silk, and cleansed of the stickiness of sea and sweat she began to feel much better.

She sat down and threw the boot at the door and Paul put his head round. 'Finished,' she said. 'It was lovely. I wish I could empty it, but——' But she wasn't up to carrying buckets anywhere.

He said, 'That's all right, I'll chuck it out later. Come on, Madame Récamier, back to the sofa, while I get the breakfast.'

'Don't cook anything for me.'

But when he brought in the tray there were two bowls of porridge on it and Anna looked at hers with queasiness. 'My grandmother used to give me this. Were you brought up on it?'

'No.' She had the sofa and he had an armchair, and the breakfast tray was on a little table between them.

There were also two mugs of coffee and Paul picked up his bowl of porridge. 'Which may be why I like it,' he said.

'Where were you brought up?' She sipped her coffee and looked at her porridge, in any case she couldn't taste either, and Paul said:

'I came out of the sea, remember.'

His grin was mischievous, teasing her, but it seemed he didn't want to talk about himself, so she asked, 'What's your play about?'

He shrugged. 'A bit of this and a bit of that. I'm just knocking ideas together.'

'Can I read it?'

'When I've written it you'll be the first.'

He was smiling at her still, and she smiled when she said, 'I don't believe there is a play. I think you're just here enjoying yourself.'

'So,' he said, 'nobody's perfect.'

There was no pinning him down on anything. A man this evasive must have something to hide, and she supposed she should be finding this sinister. What it must do was strengthen her determination not to get too involved with him. But so long as she remembered that she was only here for a few more days, and after that they would probably never see each other again, she could enjoy his company, and be thankful and grateful that he was looking after her.

While she was on St Morag's he was the dark man she had called up from the sea. When she got home then real life would take over again. One day she might find it hard to believe that any of this had ever happened. She wouldn't be coming back to St Morag's, but whenever there was a storm she would remember Paul and wonder about him.

'Eat your porridge,' he said.

He was wearing the jacket with the tear at the elbow

and she frowned at it. 'I wish I could mend that, it irritates me.'

'Then don't look at it,' he said, and she said wryly :

'That's not bad advice, what you can't mend don't worry about.'

She passed a pleasant day. She sniffed and sneezed a lot and she felt tired, but during the morning she dozed on her sofa and ate what Paul brought her, and drank what she was given. She couldn't taste any of it, but she didn't get any more whisky. If that had been produced she would have turned it down because she was keeping a cool head for tonight—no asking Paul to stay with her again and hold her hand.

If she continued improving at this rate, and if the fog didn't lift soon, she would be locking her bedroom door because she didn't trust him an inch. But for today this was a nice uncomplicated situation.

She spent all day in the parlour, with the lamp burning, the fog against the window made the room dark. They ate their meals together, and during the afternoon Anna amused herself making sketches of the island on a lined scribbling pad. Purely for pleasure. To keep as mementoes when she went home.

She sketched the harbour, the ruined street where the little shop was, houses, coves, the bull seal roaring on the beach below. She showed Paul each sketch as she finished it and he was impressed. Or he seemed to be.

He liked Big Daddy particularly. 'You really do draw very well,' he said.

She explained, 'I went to art school. I had some idea of teaching, but I found my real love when I made a wall panel.' She began to draw birds—on the rocks under the cliff where they had tried climbing, where she had met Paul for the very first time—telling him how Mr Bissell always came to the summer exhibitions of students' work and how he'd offered to consider putting her sewing on sale. 'I saw Douglas when I took my samples in,' she said, 'and I suppose I've been part of the family ever since.' She looked across at him. 'Are you part of a family?'

'No,' said Paul, making the negative amiable but final.

In the afternoon he'd brought in a paraffin heater that wasn't working, and some old newspapers that were dated two months ago. Anna pounced on them, and read the out-of-date news and articles before he could get on with his job of dismantling the stove, following a manual that he didn't seem to understand too well.

He didn't seem too sure what he was doing, and she said, 'Don't light that until I can run if it should go up.'

He was surrounded by bits and pieces and he said, 'I don't think there's much danger. By the time I've got this working you'd have recovered from a compound fracture.'

He took it away when he went to bring in tea-cum-supper, which was bread, butter, cheese and pickles and a jar of jam; and after that was cleared he produced another scribbling pad and sat at the table writing, while Anna went on with her memory sketches.

'The play?' she enquired.

'Of course.' She knew that he wouldn't show it to her, and he was writing so fast it seemed more likely to be a letter, or perhaps a diary; letters wouldn't be leaving until the fog lifted and he got his boat out. But it felt sociable, both of them sitting, working, in the warm little parlour. Outside there was the fog, and the deserted island, and the sea and night closing in, but she felt safe and secure in here.

She held up a sketch, from the top of the hill looking down towards the harbour, and he asked, 'What are you going to do with all of them?'

'Show them around,' she said promptly. 'They're my holiday pictures.'

'Who to?'

'My friends.' She had no need to be tight-mouthed, she had nothing to hide. 'Do you want to hear about them?' she asked, and he said:

'Yes.'

So she told him about Joan and Bill, who had taken her into their home when her parents were killed. He looked up at that, a brief look of sympathy, but he said nothing. About Zoe and Pete. She had so many friends, and she described them all vividly and lovingly.

Robina was the latest. After the accident Robina had been like a sister to Anna. She said, 'If I had some sketching paper instead of this lined stuff I'd do some sketches to take back as presents. It's all very picturesque and romantic-looking from a distance.'

'Shall you tell Douglas we were all alone on the island?'

She said quickly, 'Why shouldn't I tell him? It wasn't planned.'

'Wasn't it?'

He was talking rubbish, smiling at her with watchful eyes, and she said, even faster, 'Would you have any paper that doesn't have lines on it?

'Sorry,' he said. 'But if you're handing them out I'd like Big Daddy.'

'With my compliments.' She tore out the page and he came across and took it from her, and she felt that if he touched her she might cry out.

The window was open a little, drawing the warm air into the swirling fog, but the lamp and the fire suddenly seemed oppressive as though the atmosphere was becoming overcharged.

'How long do you think it will last?' she asked.

'I don't know.' He didn't touch her. He held the sheet of paper and stood looking at the window. 'There's plenty of food,' he said.

Anna wasn't worrying about a food shortage. She'd seen the cupboards, there were tins and packages. But she knew that if they were locked in here together for even a few more days they were going to get together. Paul took it for granted, and it would have been so easy for her to say, 'Share my bed tonight.'

But she mustn't, she wouldn't. She said, 'I think I'll go up,' and shook her head at the gleam in the bold black eyes.

He shrugged and smiled and asked, 'All right?' as she got up, reaching for the walking stick, feeling her ankle not too painful to take a little of her weight.

'Improving all the time,' she assured him. She was wearing thick socks, she only had one wearable boot, and she went carefully to the kitchen, where she washed hands and face in the sink and rubbed her teeth with toothpaste on a forefinger. Paul's hairbrush and comb were the limit of her beauty accessories, and although her hair was soft and pretty her face was pasty and her eyelids were puffed.

Not a very alluring sight, she thought, brushing her hair in front of the shaving mirror on the kitchen wall.

'A lamp or a candle?' asked Paul.

'A candle will do.' She wouldn't need a light burning all night. She was over her fever, and the shock of the seal hunters and the bull seal.

In the mirror she saw the matchlight flare, and then the small steady glow of the candle. 'I'll take it to your room,' he said.

'Thank you.' When she got up the stairs Paul was standing on the little landing. It was a narrow corridor, she had to pass him to reach her room at the end. She was breathing fast, hauling herself up the stairs hadn't been the easiest thing on this ankle, but she didn't need helping, she didn't want him touching her. She said, 'Goodnight.'

He put his hands on her shoulders and kissed her, running his hands slowly down her arms to her fingertips, and she felt hollow with desire. She wanted him to come to her room where the candlelight flickered, and caress her endlessly and everywhere until the candle burned out, but her ring pressed into her palm as his fingers tightened over hers, and she heard herself say, 'Goodnight,' again, and somehow she was in her room, alone.

She closed the door behind her and leaned against it, and she stayed like that for a few moments, her heart pounding like something trapped in her rib cage. There wasn't a bolt on the door, nor a key, so there would be no barring the door tonight. If Paul came to her room she hoped she would be able to send him away again, she hoped he'd go, but she was in no condition to put up much of a fight. And she wanted him, as much as he wanted her, that was the danger. She wouldn't be fighting Paul, she would be fighting herself; and she lay in bed, her body knotted with tension, rigid and restless.

If Paul came it wouldn't be her fault. She would try to send him away, but if she couldn't then perhaps he was right and it had been planned in some way that they should meet on the island, because she had never felt this kind of hunger for any man before. Perhaps there had been a calling and an answering.

She hoped he wouldn't come. But she waited, and it was a long time before she fell asleep, and her first emotion on waking was stinging disappointment.

The weather hadn't improved. The fog was still at the window and she sat up, telling herself how relieved she was that she was in bed alone. She would have felt terrible this morning if she hadn't been. Guilty about Douglas, angry with herself. This attraction between her and Paul was almost entirely physical. It had to be, because she really knew nothing about him, and she was not in the habit of falling in love with strangers.

In *love?* But this wasn't love. This was lust, and liking; although that was a heady combination. Perhaps the fog wasn't quite as thick as yesterday against the window pane. From the window her gaze fell to the dressing table and the piece of white paper on the dark mahogany.

Her ankle was getting better. She got across the room quite well, and read the note that Paul had left for her, 'You were sleeping so beautifully when I looked in that it seemed a pity to disturb you. Back for breakfast.'

So he had looked in, and he might have disturbed her, and that pleased her as though it was a compliment of sorts. She wondered where he had gone in this weather, and decided that she was fit enough to be getting breakfast ready, and hoped that she would be able to taste her first cup of coffee.

Down in the kitchen she washed and put on her jeans and sweater and her boots, rolling her ripped boot down. It was awkward, but better than walking around in Paul's socks, and anyway she wasn't moving anywhere fast.

She laid the table, and boiled the kettle, and debated over the question of whether she should cook porridge. Bacon and egg stocks were low and could make a meal later in the day. She sipped her coffee, savouring it as the flavour came faintly on her tongue, and thought how quiet the house seemed.

The clock ticked, there was no other sound at all, and she wondered again where Paul had gone. He wouldn't be just outside getting in the fuel or anything like that, or he'd hardly have left a note, and he would have been back long before this. She had no way of knowing when he had come into her room. By daylight probably, because he was just off somewhere. A before-breakfast walk, perhaps. He must be used to fog on the islands. He might just have gone for a walk.

This house was on the cliff's edge, but she wouldn't

think about that, nor about anything else that might happen out there. He would be back soon and she busied herself getting the porridge up to the simmer, stirring and fussing, watching the clock and trying to hold down her growing concern.

When she went to the back door and opened it the freezing fog was as clammy as wet cotton wool, and as she peered out she thought—going blind would be like this, and felt a flutter of panic in her throat.

Where *was* Paul? She went back into the kitchen, sitting at the table, twisting her fingers in an agony of frustration and anxiety. He'd been gone the best part of an hour at least, and *where*, for heaven's sake? She didn't even know which direction to start looking, and she couldn't walk far on this wretched ankle and nobody could see through the fog. Had he taken a torch? She didn't find one when she went through the kitchen drawers and cupboards. The big torch was still at her cottage, and she didn't know if he had another. She took the lamp upstairs and lit it, and placed it in her bedroom window, where it might act as a faint beacon. From up here she could see the fog was patchy and dispersing.

If it cleared a little more she would go searching for Paul. That might be stupid, but she didn't believe she could just sit around the house worrying.

By now she was nearly frantic, because something must have happened. She opened the front door, and shut it quickly. There was nothing out there but the rough sparse grass of the cliff top before it fell sheer on to Spanish Sands. Paul wouldn't have gone that way in this weather.

Anna went to the back door and listened to the crashing of the waves over the rocks and the screaming cries of birds and shouted, 'Paul, where are you?' As the density of the fog had thinned sound was carrying again. He might hear her and she called his name again, venturing out a little way, peering through the floating fog but making sure she didn't lose sight of the house.

Before she tried tramping around she would have to do something about her flapping boot. He'd said there were no needles and thread around, but she could surely find something to go round it, if it was only a piece of string.

'*Paul!*' she screamed at the top of her voice, cupping her hands to tunnel the sound, and he answered her:

'Coming!'

She dropped her hands to her sides in a relief that made her feel almost faint for a moment, then exasperation prickled through her veins and she shrieked, 'Where have you been?'

The fog made him seem abnormally tall when he loomed up, a dark fuzzy figure, and she stumbled back to the house, her boot flopping round her ankles, demanding querulously, 'What the hell have you been doing?'

'Miss me?' he asked, and he sounded maddeningly cheerful so that she would have given a great deal not to have been caught out there, screaming her head off.

She went into the kitchen and sat down huffily at the table. She hoped the porridge had burned—he could get his own breakfast.

He put her suitcase on the table, and another bag down too, and said, 'I went to collect a few things for you.'

'To the *cottage?*' she squeaked.

'Where else?'

'That was a crazy risk.'

'Not really. I stayed on the road.' But it was still a risk.

Anna clicked the case open. There were clothes folded, and on top of them lay her sketch pad and pencils, and her sewing case. Her toilet-make-up bag was tucked in at the side. She was glad to see them all, they were what she needed to speed her recovery: a choice of her own clothes, and the make-up bag; and work to do if she wanted to work.

She said, 'Thank you,' and looked down at the other bag, a canvas carrier that Paul must have taken along with him. Her shoes were in that, he seemed to have brought the lot, and she said, 'You've decided I'm staying here?'

'Aren't you?' He gave the porridge a stir and took it off the gas ring, and she said:

'I'll have to, won't I? Until the fog lifts.'

'It is lifting.'

He sat down, waiting for the kettle to boil, and she might as well wait for a fresh cup herself, this was quite cold. She said abruptly, 'I'll be glad when it's gone, there's something about the fog here that scares me, it's like——' She paused, biting on her lip, and after a moment he said:

'Going blind?'

He *did* know. She *had* talked in her sleep. As her temperature soared the nightmares had gone on. He met her enquiring gaze steadily now. The wet fog had made his thick dark hair curl. He hadn't shaved before he went out and the shadow showed, giving him an unkempt appearance, but he still looked able to cope with anything.

Anna asked, 'What did I say?'

He kept his eyes on her, as though no expression or gesture was going to escape him, and told her, 'You said "I'm not going blind, I'm all right," over and over. Was it after the car crash?' She nodded. 'Tell me about it,' he said.

It seemed that she couldn't put it out of her mind as easily as she had hoped. She had run away to get things clear, but she was still troubled and scared.

'There was a time when the doctors weren't sure I hadn't damaged a nerve or something,' she told him. She rubbed her temples very lightly with her fingertips, because she could remember those headaches so vividly that it was nearly like one pounding away now.

'And?' Paul prompted quietly.

'I hadn't,' she said eagerly. 'I'm all right, but that's really why I came here. To be away from everybody who knew me, to see if I could have faced life by myself if I'd had to.' She forced a smile, but her lips were so stiff that she was sure it was more like a grimace. 'I didn't expect to find the island to be deserted, of course, but I thought if there was anywhere I could get myself together it would be on St Morag's.'

He interrupted her, 'Maybe I'm being thick, but where does Douglas fit into this bit about facing life by yourself?' And then she had to tell him everything, although she couldn't look at him while she spoke. She took her sketchpad out of the case and turned the pages and pretended to be looking at that.

'I—I heard him talking. I didn't know until I was out of hospital that they'd been worried about my eyes. I heard the family talking about how good it was that the tests were all clear, and Douglas saying he would still have married me if they hadn't been.'

She was at the sketch she had made of Douglas. 'But that it would have been a hellish life,' she finished.

Paul said nothing. When she looked across at him from the copy of Douglas's unlived-in face he was frowning, and she said, 'Well, it would have been, wouldn't it? And I'm not absolutely sure it was Douglas who said that, it could have been his father. They sound a lot alike.'

She didn't want to turn Douglas into a villain. He was a kind man, who loved her, and it had been an appalling situation for him.

She went on defending him. 'I'd have been a real drag if my eyesight had been affected. It's close work, mine, and I'm starting to make a name for myself. I've had two exhibitions, I'm one of their best sellers in the Galleries. If my eyes had been even a little bit affected I'd have been so sorry for myself, I'd have been unbearable to live with.'

'Are they?' Paul asked, still quietly, and she said shrilly:

'*No!* Well, I've got this cold in my head now so they look a bit bleary, but I can see perfectly. After I knew there'd been a risk I spoke to the doctor who was in charge of my case and he was quite specific that I was fine. No danger.'

Paul went on looking at her, and it seemed that the words were being dragged through her lips. 'I overworked when I got back to work, there were a lot of orders from the exhibition and once I thought,' she gulped, 'I thought my eyes seemed to blur. But I was overtired and—well, that's when I decided to come up here for a holiday.' She rubbed her forehead now, fingertips groping round from her temples, and again she tried to smile. 'I suppose that's going to be one of my nightmares for a long time.'

'We all have them,' said Paul, and when he smiled Anna stopped rubbing her forehead to ask:

'What kind of nightmares do you have?'

'Next time I scream in my sleep you wake me and I'll tell you,' he said, and she laughed spontaneously.

'I wake you, do I? If I did that in the middle of the night mightn't you get the wrong ideas?'

'Of course not.' He got up and went to the kettle. 'Any ideas I got would be very good ones,' he said. 'I'm a great ideas man. We could discuss one or two of them now if you liked.'

'I would not like.' She felt much better for talking, glad he was back, pleased to have her things. 'I sat down to drink that and then I started wondering what I should do if you'd fallen off a cliff,' she said.

'Wait till the fog cleared and then come looking for me?' he suggested.

'Certainly not before.' She put two teaspoons of coffee in the mugs, picked up the steaming kettle, and he said: 'I do admire a practical woman. I brought your needles and thread along so you could mend my coat.'

The porridge was so lumpy it was inedible, and he cooked bacon and eggs while Anna invisibly darned the sleeve of his jacket, teasing a few threads of the fibre from the turned-in material and darning with them. Then she reinforced the repair with one of her own long chestnut-coloured hairs, making tiny stitches, and Paul watched with interest. 'Wouldn't you like one of mine?' he suggested. 'I think we'd mingle rather well.'

'Too coarse,' she said promptly, and he grinned.

'I'll bet Douglas has lovely silky hair.'

As it happened Douglas did have silky hair, and smooth skin. There was nothing coarse or tough about the man she was supposed to be marrying, but she had told Paul enough about Douglas for one morning, so she sniffed and said, 'My taste and smell seem to be improving—— You're burning the bacon!'

Now she had her pad, with the sketches for the Spanish Sands wall panel, she wanted to get to work on that again, and when the table was cleared after breakfast she settled down and played around with ideas happily for about half an hour.

'I've got something for you,' said Paul, coming back into the kitchen from upstairs.

'What?'

'Inspiration.'

He put a round heavy coin on the table, and Anna picked it up, gasping, 'It's a doubloon, isn't it?' The date was a few years before the Armada. There would have been coins like this on board the sunken galleon, although of course this was a copy. She would work it into her panel, and she examined it with fascinated delight.

'A present for you,' said Paul.

'It isn't genuine?' She was alarmed for a moment, but he grinned:

'Could I afford the real thing?' Then she smiled.

'Thank you. It's marvellous. Whenever I look at this I'll remember Spanish Sands.'

'And the dark man you called up in the storm?'

'Of course.' She might have called him up in the storm for all she knew about him. He could have been a demon lover. His charm was spellbinding.

'The fog's clearing,' he said.

'Is it?' When Anna looked at the window she was surprised. She had been so engrossed with her sketches she hadn't noticed.

'I could probably get the boat out tomorrow. If that's what you want.'

Her breath caught in her throat. She wanted to stay here for a long time, and not worry about tomorrow nor about anyone but themselves. He sat on the edge of the table, looking down at her, and it was all she could do not to turn and cling to him. That could be her answer. If she did that there would be no need for any words.

She might have been rash enough, if he hadn't got up suddenly and walked across to the window. All the nerves in her body clamoured for him, but she couldn't speak, and she couldn't follow. She put down the doubloon and went on examining it closely, as though she was trying to memorise the design, and Paul said, 'I think I'll go and check on the boat.'

'Is that safe?'

'Yes—look. It's breaking up, there's a wind rising. You'd better not come, had you?'

The boat was in a small protected bay, McNab's Cove, named after a fisherman who had been dead two hundred years, only a short distance away. But the scramble down would have been more than she could manage just yet. She said, 'I'll stay here.'

'Please stay,' he said quietly. He knew that she wasn't promising beyond tomorrow, and she looked away from the appeal in his eyes. When he came back she would say, 'Before I let myself in for a love affair I'd need to know a little more about you than the nothing I know now.'

She would need to be very sure of her feelings before she agreed to stay here in this house with Paul, for the rest of her holiday. As things stood she could go back home and face Douglas, still wearing his ring, and probably life would go on again in the old way.

But if she stayed she would take off the ring, even if she left at the end of the fortnight and never saw Paul again. Once they became lovers she would be vulnerable. Paul would be able to hurt her. She would be completely in his power, because she was under his spell now and he had hardly laid a hand on her.

She had to find out more about him. She had never gone spying and prying before, and it was a grubby feeling, opening the doors upstairs until she found the room Paul used, and then starting to go through cupboards and drawers.

She opened the wardrobe first, and saw the kind of clothes she expected hanging on the hangers. There might be something here, an address might help, but she couldn't force herself to slip her fingers into the pockets. Clothes were so personal. They *looked* like him, and touching them she felt as mean and furtive as a sneak thief.

She closed the wardrobe and went over to the wash-basin table, with a marble top and two drawers. There were a couple of scribbling pads in the first drawer, and on top of them were newspaper cuttings. At a quick glance the cuttings all seemed concerned with crime, robberies mostly, one case of blackmail, and Anna told herself that his play was obviously a thriller. But her eyes darted for names and locations, seeking a link between them that she dreaded to find.

And there was a letter, with no envelope and no home address at the top, just the date, the sixth of last month. 'Darling Paul,' it began, and ended, 'Always and ever your Gemma.'

It was a passionate letter, making it crystal clear that Gemma was crazy about him, and that when he had said nobody was waiting to hear from him he had lied.

Anna dropped the letter as though it was red hot, and shut the drawer. She didn't need to see any more. Gemma had told her how far she could trust Paul.

'Anna!' she heard him calling, and she made a hasty dash for the door, gritting her teeth at the twinge in her ankle, frantic to get on to the landing before he came up the stairs and caught her coming out of his room.

CHAPTER SIX

Anna reached the top of the stairs as Paul appeared at the bottom. She didn't think he could have seen which door she had come through. All he said was, 'Ah, there you are,' and she said:

'That was quick.'

He'd come back for a bag. There was food on the boat he'd recalled and he might as well bring it up to the house. 'You're all right?' he asked. Anna was breathless and possibly pale and he was looking intently at her, and she made her voice extra hearty assuring him that she was fine, of course, getting healthier by the minute.

'Good,' he said. 'I'll see you in about an hour,' and he had gone, while she was still clutching the handrail at the top of the stairs. She stayed clutching it for a few moments, hearing doors shut below, then she went into her own bedroom and sat down on the bed.

The lamp was still burning in the window. When she felt a little steadier she must turn it out, and there was really no reason why she should be shaking. The letter should have been no shock. Of course there were women in Paul's life.

Probably dozens of them. But Anna didn't want to end writing letters like that to a man who was sleeping around. Poor Gemma, she thought, loving a man she could never trust, and she thought how lucky she was to have Douglas waiting.

She went to the window and turned down the flame of the lamp, until it guttered out and a thin wisp of smoke rose from the glass of the globe. Outside the fog was going and the wind was rising, wailing like a banshee; and Anna could have howled with it, she felt so depressed. She was being sensible, making her head rule her heart, but it was a hard decision and she hoped she wasn't going to regret it one day.

When Paul came back she was sitting at the kitchen table, sketching. She'd leave Spanish Sands until she got home. Now she was copying yesterday's sketches of scenes around the island, and trying to keep her mind on them.

He tipped about a dozen tins on the table. The round ones rolled, she got a tin of pineapple chunks in her lap, and he asked, 'What shall we have for dinner?'

'How's the boat?' she asked. She put the pineapple chunks back on the table, and picked up a baked beans from the floor.

'Fine.'

'And the weather?'

'Not bad. The wind's up, but it always sounds worse up here.' He took newspapers from the bottom of the bag. 'That's a bit out of date, but it's still worth reading.'

'Is there any chance of getting away today?'

'It's too late today. Anyhow, the plane doesn't go till tomorrow.' There were two planes a week in the wintertime from Carra to the mainland, and four ferries; but it might be dark today before he could land her, and then he had to come back. She admitted he had a point, but she would have given a great deal to be able to leave right now.

'What's the hurry?' he asked, and he came behind her chair leaning over her, his breath warm on her face. Anna jerked back and the chair slipped and he caught her, and turned her as she twisted away from him, pulling her hard against him. His mouth came down on hers, stifling, overpowering, his hand was on her breast and desire ran raging through her. She was on fire for him and she fought herself. He was not taking her like this. It was not happening this way, she would not let it happen. When he lifted his head from her lips she spat through clenched teeth, 'No, I will not!'

But Paul hovered over her like a hawk, his talons in her flesh. 'How does it feel when Douglas makes love to you?' and Anna knew that she had never been stirred so deeply before. Every inch of her tingled. Flesh and bone. Little electric shocks were still running up and down her spine, and her body ached with longing. She felt she would never be free of pain until she let him love her, and this passion was pain. Tearing away from him was like ripping herself in two.

Douglas, she thought, *Douglas* ... She couldn't even remember what he looked like, but she had to keep thinking of Douglas. 'Let me go,' she begged, and he said hoarsely :

'Take that damn ring off. Stay with me.'

She closed her eyes and then she could say, 'I don't want to stay. I want to go home.' Oh, she was scared now. She was terrified that she couldn't stop him. She knew how strong he was and she had half promised this in a dozen ways. She shrank within his grip, cowering, her eyes still closed, and she felt his hold loosening until his fingers were only in her hair.

He lifted her hair and she knew he kissed it and she was shaken by the violence of her heartbeats. Then he said, 'All right. Tomorrow.'

His voice sounded rueful, but he was taking rejection easy enough. He grinned as she stared at him. 'You can stop fluttering, my bonny bird. Taking 'em by force isn't my style.'

He was laughing at her and that stopped her fluttering. It also made her feel a fool, and after a moment she managed to ask : 'Can I go to the cottage?'

He might bring the boat to the harbour. If he wouldn't

she could stay in the cottage for another day or two and start flashing her S.O.S. from the window. Now that the fog was clearing surely the boats would see her.

'Can you walk two miles?' he asked.

Anna had forgotten her ankle, although she was standing on it. She shook her head and sat down, and Paul started stacking the tins he had brought into the pantry. 'Shall you go straight home?'

So he did mean to get her off the island, she was relieved about that, and she said, 'I think I'll go to a hotel for a few days. If I turned up looking like this they wouldn't think my holiday had done me much good.'

The rest of the day dragged by, so slowly that she could have thrown something at the clock on the wall with its silly smug face. Half a dozen times she could have sworn it must have stopped, but it went on ticking and she went on sketching, and doing a little dusting, and making a macaroni cheese for their midday meal.

They ate together, but it wasn't the same as the other meals, because she felt that Paul was playing cat and mouse with her. Circling her, ready to pounce, even when he was sitting at the table eating macaroni cheese.

She read the old newspaper and they talked about the articles and the out-of-date news, and all the time the room was overcrowded with him. When he looked at her it was as though he was touching her, and when he took the salt pot from her and his fingers brushed hers her hand went boneless.

He knew that. He said, 'You're making a mistake, leaving.'

'I don't think so.' She sat very straight and stiff, stabbing macaroni with a fork. 'I'm getting married at Easter,' she said coldly, 'and I don't have your standards.'

'What are my standards?'

'Anybody who's around, I should think,' she said tartly, and Paul made a gesture of despair.

'You've been listening to gossip.'

'What?'

'Joke,' he explained, and she said:

'Sorry.' But she couldn't relax nor laugh. Some of her conduct had been provocative and she couldn't blame him for thinking she was easy. But she wasn't. It had been the weird loneliness of St Morag's that had thrown her out of character. It had seemed another dimension up here, as though Paul had been waiting for her and had known she would come and now they were together for ever.

But the letter had recalled the world outside where Douglas was waiting for her, and a girl called Gemma thought she was waiting for Paul. He didn't care. He would keep Anna here, sharing bed and board, perhaps for as long as she would stay. But he would have done the same with any passably attractive girl who had landed on the shore.

That was the difference in their standards. To her the idea of lovemaking without love was degrading, and if he didn't take her to Carra tomorrow she would get back to her cottage somehow, if she had to crawl half the way.

'Who's cooking supper?' he asked.

Supper tonight. Anna wouldn't put it past him to produce another bottle of wine, and the full seduction scene. She said, 'I might as well. What time can we leave in the morning?'

'Early as you like. As soon as it's light.'

'Thank you,' she said. 'I'd like to go early,' and she was silenced by the penetrating look he gave her. It was brief, he smiled almost immediately.

'Part of the service,' he said, but it gave her the feeling that he wasn't going to let her get away as easily as that.

She hoped she hadn't piqued his masculine pride, set

herself up as a challenge. She was almost sure he wouldn't use force, but she remembered him when the seal hunters came, and she felt that he could be a dangerous man.

If only the night was over! She would lie awake tonight terrified, she knew she would, at the very least. At the worst she could find herself battling like a Victorian heroine. It could be an ugly night. It could be a terrifying night.

Or it could be nothing. But she would still lie listening for the creaking board on the landing, and watching for the door that she couldn't bolt to slowly open.

Unless she took a sleeping pill. If she did that, and pushed the chest of drawers up against the door, and maybe the bed too, that might get her a peaceful night. Paul had brought the pills in her make-up bag back from the cottage, and tonight she would take one. Better still, if she could get Paul to take a couple of them and make sure that he slept long and soundly.

It wasn't a serious plan when it first came into her mind while she was looking at the pills in her hand. They weren't that small, it would be risky putting them whole into something. She went on thinking about it, as a mental exercise. She crushed one and it tasted bitter, so it would need a strong flavour to hide it. A really large whisky perhaps, but she couldn't get the whisky bottle and start pouring, and how would she manage to slip in her Mickey Finn and wouldn't the white powder float in sinister fashion on top?

In food about the strongest flavour she could lay hands on was the tin of curry powder. Paul had brought a tin of corned beef back from the boat this morning. She'd thought of making some sort of hash with that, but she would make a curry. She liked curry, and there were onions and fruit and several packets of quick cooking rice in the cupboard. She'd think about the sleeping pills, but it wasn't a bad idea.

Before she went down again to the kitchen she cleansed her face with cleansing milk and rubbed in a little moisturiser and put on a touch of lipstick. Then she brushed her hair hard with her own brush, because there was no need to go around looking so washed-out. Suddenly she felt more confident, more in charge.

Paul was out until darkness fell. The curry was maturing in a frying pan with a plate on top, and it was hot enough to take the skin off the roof of her mouth, but all in a good cause if she did decide to add the two powdered pills to his portion. She had them in a spoon among a clutter of cutlery and bowls on the table beside the stove. It would only take a second's sleight of hand to tip them in.

It would have been better if she could have done that in advance and had the two plates ready, but she wasn't sure whether curry powder might evaporate the power or something. She had never tried dosing anyone in secret before.

The lamp was lit and standing in the middle of the table, and she had gone back to her sketch pad. She almost tore out the pages of Paul, the sight of him gave her the jitters, but it was a striking face and she might still use it for her panel.

It was Douglas she was working on tonight. The sketch that hadn't satisfied her before. Now she put in shading and spent time and trouble coaxing it into life and it was improving. His mother might like to have it, and perhaps one of Robina too.

Anna turned another page and began to sketch Robina, with her long straight fair hair and her childish face. Robina would never believe it if she knew what Anna had been up to since she last saw her, Anna couldn't see herself confiding in Robina. Nor in Douglas. Nor, really, in anybody. Even Zoe would say she must have been an idiot to get herself under the same roof as a man she had to knock unconscious.

She heard Paul—it had to be Paul—open the back door, and applied herself assiduously to her sketching. When he came into the kitchen she glanced up briefly through the fall in her hair, and said, 'Oh, hello,' very cool and casual.

'Hello,' he said. He looked over her shoulder. 'Who's that?'

'Robina. Douglas's sister.'

She had told him all about Robina when she was talking about her friends. 'She looks about sixteen,' he commented.

'She's a year older than me,' said Anna, wondering why she was bothering to tell him that.

'Led a sheltered life, has she?' Paul was still examining the sketch, and she put down her pencil because she couldn't go on drawing now.

'I suppose so.'

'Like Douglas?'

Douglas hadn't lived a sheltered life. Douglas travelled all over the world for the Galleries.

Paul pulled the pad from under her hand and turned to Douglas's sketch. A quirk of his eyebrows acknowledged her recent work on it, but his expression was wry. 'He's not right for you.'

'How would you know?' She glared at him and met the glittering eyes over the devilish smile and said, 'Please don't let's quarrel. I'd like to part friends. I really would.'

'Has it been nice knowing me?' He stood with his arms folded, and she said:

'Interesting. Yes.'

'It has, hasn't it? Interesting. We must do it again some time.' In the lamplight he had the haughty face of a conquistador, the face of a dark demon. 'I'll call you,' he said.

'You do that.' Anna hadn't given him her phone number, but she'd talked about Joan and Bill and the

Laurels Guest House. He could find the number. But not on St Morag's, and he probably wouldn't bother after she'd gone.

She went to the stove and poured boiling water from the kettle into a saucepan and put in the packages of rice. 'Do you like curry?' she asked.

'Yes.'

That was as well. 'It's nearly ready.'

As he washed at the sink with his back to her, she spooned the curry on to two plates. She was still undecided about the pills and then she thought, they're not that powerful, they won't hurt him, he's strong as an ox. And she stirred one portion with the spoon holding the crushed powder.

Paul went to the table and she busied herself with the dishing up of the meal, still at the stove. He was holding the sketch pad, looking at one sketch with concentrated attention, and she put the two dishes of rice and curry down on the table and sat down and picked up her folk.

Her mouth was dry and her stomach was churning. She wondered if Lucretia Borgia used to feel this way, and had a horrible feeling that she might start giggling. What a daft thing she was doing! It would be hysterically funny if she was away from here. It was a tale she might tell months ahead, naming no names and no places, and to girl friends only. Douglas and his parents would think she was Lucretia Borgia.

She mixed a little rice with a little curry and forked it into her mouth and it tasted like pure curry powder to her. At the same moment Paul got his first mouthful and asked, 'What's in this?'

Anna gulped in cooling air, and gasped out the words, 'Corned beef, onions, curry powder, sultanas.'

He wasn't going to eat it, and she couldn't blame him. But he leaned across and changed plates and she felt the blood draining out of her face. She must look a picture of guilt, goggling and gulping, and she struggled to make her expression merely one of slight surprise and hoped that was how she sounded, just surprised, asking him, 'Why did you do that?'

'No difference, is there?' Perhaps he thought hers was milder.

'No,' she said.

'Then what does it matter?'

If it didn't matter why had he done it? He must have seen her and all she could do now was try to bluff it out. 'It doesn't,' she said. 'I seem to have overdone the seasoning in both.'

'It's not too bad if you mix it with the rice, and a glass of water might help.'

He filled two glasses under the hand pump at the sink and while he was doing that he wasn't looking at her and she might have managed to switch the plates back again. But he would probably have caught her leaning across the table, and neither her hands nor her nerves were steady enough for split-second reactions.

Then he sat down and started to eat. She had to put on a show. She ate a lot of rice, and as little curry as possible, and then she said, 'It's too hot for me. I've really overdone the curry powder, and anyhow I'm not hungry.'

'Come on,' he urged. 'Just a little more.'

He was watching her too closely for comfort. He was always too close for comfort, and she ate another couple of forksful and thought, it's back to plan one. I take the pills and get a sound night's sleep after I've barricaded my door.

She said, 'I'm having an early night. I've still got this beastly cold, and I think I'd better get a good night's rest.'

'Ready for tomorrow?' He sounded as though that was reasonable, and she said, 'You are taking me back tomorrow, aren't you?'

'Yes, of course.' He sounded as though he meant it. A

small request that would certainly be granted. He leaned forward, looking grave. 'If I were you,' he said, 'I'd get off to bed now, you could be getting a temperature again.'

Anna's pallor had gone and her cheeks were flushed. She touched a cheekbone and it felt almost as hot as her mouth and throat. She pushed the plate aside and said, 'It's the curry. It's too strong.'

'Packs quite a punch,' Paul agreed. Oh yes, he knew, and she hoped it was stress and curry powder that were making her head swim, not the sleeping pills starting to work already, because it would be awful if she flaked out down here.

'Goodnight, then,' she said, although it was not quite six o'clock. Paul got up and lit a candle for her and she said, 'I'll take it, thank you.'

'Sleep well,' he said.

The cooler air in her bedroom cleared her head a little, and she put the candle on the dressing table and looked at her reflection in the spotted mirror. She looked flushed and wild-eyed. By candlelight and with the dark old-fashioned room behind her she looked like someone in a Dracula movie. Tomorrow night she would be in a hotel room, with central heating and a bathroom all her own if she was lucky, and a door that closed and locked.

Tomorrow she would be in a different world. But tonight she was here, and it would be ridiculous to start piling furniture up against the door that didn't lock.

On the other hand Paul did wander in and out of her room, and might not think the game was over yet, and there ought to be locks on the bedroom doors.

The chest of drawers was a heavy piece, and she mustn't make a noise. She eased the drawers out, but it was hard work lowering them silently to the floor. Then she dragged and pushed the chest and set it flush against the door.

With the drawers back in place, it was quite a barrier.

The door could be forced open, but not without a lot of noise and effort, and she couldn't see Paul literally crashing his way in.

By now she was feeling distinctly muzzy, and her fingers fumbled as she got out of her clothes and into pyjamas. She crawled under the duvet and lay panting. She'd forgotten to blow out the candle, but it was safe enough, the holder had a wide base to catch dripping wax. Maybe she'd get up in a few minutes and douse it, but her eyelids were too heavy for a little candlelight to make any difference, and her arms and legs were too heavy.

She sank down down into darkness, and knew nothing but silence and dark until a hammer began to beat in her brain, and she opened her eyes in a narrow slit, and white light assailed her.

The banging went on. It wasn't in her head. It was on the door and Paul was shouting, 'Anna, are you all right?'

'Yes.' He was still banging the door so perhaps he hadn't heard that. 'Yes!' she called again.

'Open this door!'

'Why?'

'Because you've slept for fourteen hours and I want to see if you're fit to travel.' Her eyes opened wider at that and she remembered. 'You want to leave here today, don't you?' Paul was asking her.

'Yes.' She sat up groggily, and got out of bed, feeling her way along the bed reaching for the support of the chest of drawers. 'Wait a bit.'

She had to take the drawers out again and this time they came down with a bump. Then she had to shove them out of the way and drag the chest from the door. As soon as there was room for the door to open a few inches Paul put his head round it. He grinned, surveying her handiwork. 'You did go to a lot of trouble. Was it to stop me getting in or you getting out?' She surveyed him with lacklustre eyes and he enquired, 'How many sleeping pills did you put in the curry?'

'How did you know?' He did know, so there was no sense denying it.

'I knew you had them,' he said, 'and I saw you acting shifty in the shaving mirror.' Of course, his back had been towards her when he'd been at the sink, but the mirror had been in front of him. 'All that curry powder had to be masking something,' he went on. 'The way you looked when I switched the plates it could have been rat poison. If we'd had any rat poison.'

'So it was stupid.' She'd known that all along, and she scowled at him because he had made her act so stupidly. 'But I didn't fancy spending half the night fighting you off.'

'You flatter yourself,' he said cheerfully. 'Have you seen yourself?'

'Look, will you get your head out of that doorway and let me get dressed?'

'That's all right,' his grin was maddening, 'I don't do much ravishing in the mornings.'

'Oh, shut up!' She reached to slam the door but he shut it before she could, and then she grinned herself. What a carry-on! It was almost like the beginning again, except that it was the end, and she probably had to hurry to have any chance of catching that plane.

She brought her case downstairs with her, and smelled coffee as she opened the kitchen door. She hoped Paul wouldn't go on about the sleeping pills. She still had a thick head, the coffee was very welcome, and she wasn't up to cut-and-thrust talk. She finished her packing downstairs, and ate a little cereal, then said apologetically, 'I can't manage any more. I think I'll wait.'

'Until you're in civilisation?'

'Yes.'

'Do you want to call at the cottage?'

Her winter coat was still there and Zoe's bedroll, and she supposed she should lock the door and fasten the shutters. 'Please,' she said, and went to get her oilskin that was hanging in the little passageway to the back door.

She had a slight pang of regret leaving this house. She looked back at it with mixed feelings, but regret was among them because she sighed as she followed Paul, who was carrying her bags and striding on ahead.

In about ten minutes they reached the cove where the boat was anchored. There was no beach here and the sea was always deep. It was a natural harbour, but too small to take more than one or two fishing boats. The one boat bobbing there was a little boat with an outboard motor.

They paddled out in the rubber dinghy and as they chugged out of the cove, skirting the coastline, Anna almost wished she had been staying. It would have been fun to go sailing. She asked, 'Is this your boat?' and Paul said:

'It goes with the house.'

'You're getting it free?'

'I'm keeping it in good nick. Sort of caretaker.'

Sailing as close as this the island looked big, and the cliffs towering high. He took them between the rocks and if she had been staying she might have asked if he would teach her how to handle a boat.

It was cold still, bitterly cold, and faint traces of fog still lingered so that when they came round into the harbour it was as bleak and ghostly as ever.

Anna wasted no time in the cottage. She rolled up the sleeping bag and picked up her coat, and hurried back along the jetty and down the well worn stone steps, considering for the first time the possibility of selling. The offers had come from summer visitors, possibly hoping to make a home here. In winter time they would see it differently, but she wouldn't be back, in winter or summer.

She was leaving for the last time, and it was almost as silent a journey as her trip out from Carra. Paul kept the boat on course, a tall dark figure at the wheel, and Anna sat with her own quiet thoughts.

There were things to watch—the birds, other boats passing them, the isle of Carra, growing larger as they neared it and finally slipped into harbour.

By contrast with St Morag's Carra seemed a bustling place, because there were half a dozen fishing boats and another small dinghy anchored here. And the few men and women on the quayside looked like a crowd.

Anna faced Paul, her luggage around her, standing on Carra. 'Can you manage?' he asked.

'Yes, thank you.'

She didn't want him coming any further with her. She could enquire about the ferry here, or get herself to the sandy beach that was the island's airport at low water, and check her chances on today's plane to Glasgow. Failing either there was a very small hotel and houses that would lodge a traveller.

She said, 'Goodbye, it's been a holiday I won't forget in a hurry,' and held out a hand. She didn't want Paul kissing her, her hand was as much a barrier as a farewell gesture, but he took it and shook it.

'Goodbye,' he said, like a cheerful stranger. 'See you.'

She hoped he didn't mean it, and she smiled and turned away at the exact moment that he did. She didn't look towards the sea again. She kept her face resolutely turned to the land.

Her stay in Glasgow was everything she needed. She booked into a comfortable hotel and pampered herself with a few days of complete relaxation. All the other guests seemed to be middle-aged, and she answered the inquisitive ones with the honest answer that she had been ill and she was here convalescing.

She walked round the shops and the art galleries and she sent postcards home. One was telling Douglas that she missed him and was looking forward to seeing him again, and that was the truth. But she stayed until the end of her second week and then, armed with small presents and feeling quite her old self again, she arrived at the Laurels Guest House by taxi from the station.

She hadn't let anyone know her exact time of arrival. She wanted to slip quietly back, not to be met at the station and questioned about her holiday. She wanted to unpack and wash away the grime and strain of the journey, then change into fresh clothes and then ring up Douglas and say, 'I'm here!'

Joan was the one who got her first, because Joan was in the downstairs front room when the taxi drew up outside. Anna saw the curtains pulled back and Joan was out on the pavement while Anna was still settling up and being helped out with her luggage.

Joan gave her a friendly peck on the cheek and took the rolled up sleeping bag and said, 'We didn't expect you till tomorrow. You said probably Sunday.'

'I changed my mind and I managed to get a flight.'

'Well, it's done you good.' Joan looked at her approvingly, edging through the front door, her arms full of sleeping bag. 'You look much better.'

Thanks to the luxury of the last few days Anna's cold was no more than an occasional sniff now, and her ankle only ached if she walked too far or turned it awkwardly.

'Come in for a cup of tea?' Joan invited, stopping in the hall and looking towards the door of her kitchen, but Anna said:

'I'll think I'll go straight up,' so Joan followed with the sleeping bag.

'What was the weather like?' she asked.

'Rough,' said Anna.

'I thought so,' said Joan with gloomy satisfaction. 'It's been bad down here. I've said to Bill more than one night, "I'll bet Anna's feeling the cold up on that little island".'

'The nights weren't cold,' Anna might have said. 'We always had a fire burning and sometimes things got too hot for comfort.' But she didn't say anything at all. She gave a faint chuckle, which was what Joan expected, and then said, 'Yes, it was bleak.'

The opening buds on the camellia were bright pink, and there were several letters waiting for her on her table. She put down her luggage and went through the mail while Joan filled the kettle, plugged it in and switched on. Three were from friends, one was from the Inland Revenue and the rest were assorted circulars.

When she ripped open the last envelope, glanced inside, and dropped it on the table, Joan said, 'Well, come on, tell me about it.'

'My holiday?'

'Anything. I was thinking about your holiday, but is there anything else to tell?'

Anna smiled, 'Like what? Yes, it was a nice holiday. I needed it—the break. But it was quite a shock when I got there because St Morag's is nearly deserted. Some of the houses are summer lettings, but most of the crofters and fishermen have left or died. It's happening a lot. It's very sad.' She started putting the letters from friends back in their envelopes. 'I came back to Glasgow after a few days,' she said. 'Didn't you get my card?'

'No.'

'That's the post for you. It'll be arriving on Monday, I expect. I've got a very small thing for you here.'

She found the little box that contained the Celtic dirk brooch she had bought for Joan, and Joan pinned it on her jacket and discovered that the amethyst-coloured stone on the hilt matched the heather fleck in her tweed suit. 'It's lovely,' said Joan, beaming. 'It looks a treat. Now can I bring you up anything to eat?'

'Thanks, but I expect I'll be eating with Douglas,' said Anna. 'Perhaps I'd better phone him right away.' The two went downstairs together and Anna dialled the Galleries' number.

'I'm back,' she said, when she was put straight through to Douglas, and it was good to hear his voice, saying how pleased he was that the holiday was over and how he'd be along the moment the Galleries closed. He couldn't leave before, but she understood that, and anyhow she wanted time to change. She blew him a kiss down the phone and knew he couldn't return it, because there was nearly always someone else in his office and Douglas was a dignified man, inherently incapable of playing the fool.

She was glad to be home. Her work was lying around and she was even more eager to get back to it than she had been when she came out of hospital, because now she really was fit and well again, just the way she had been before the accident happened.

If she tried she was sure she could cut out those weeks from her mind, forget the accident, forget St Morag's, pretend it was the night after Douglas's mother's birthday party and Douglas was coming for her, and she loved and trusted him and there had never been a time when she had doubted him.

She unpacked her case, putting most of the clothes into the laundry basket. She hadn't told Joan the full story of St Morag's, and she wouldn't mention Paul to Douglas either because he simply wasn't important. He had been there, but there was no need to emphasise that they had been the only man and woman on the island, still less that they had been living in the same house. She wouldn't lie, but she wouldn't go into details like that if there was any way of avoiding them.

Douglas did get away a few minutes early, but she was ready and waiting and slowly sipping her third cup of tea. She heard him running up the stairs and called, 'Come in!' before he could knock on the door.

When he came into the room she flew into his arms, and returned his kiss with an ardour that surprised and delighted him. He didn't have to ask, 'Missed me?' although he did, and she said, 'All the time. Now come and tell me what's been happening while I've been away.'

She sat down on the sofa and patted the place beside her. 'How's the family?' she asked.

'They're all right.'

'The Galleries? Anything new?'

'No.' He would have preferred kissing her again, she was looking beautiful, but in his arms she went on with her questions as though she had been away a long time, and he found himself describing some etchings that had arrived at the Galleries and telling her that his mother was having the drawing room redecorated.

Anna listened attentively, because she wanted to talk about her life here and forget St Morag's. But Douglas asked at last, 'How was it on the island?'

'I cheated,' she told him. 'I went back to Glasgow. It was very bleak on St Morag's.'

'Still the same folk?'

'Not so many of them.' She was seeing it all again, the shells of buildings, the empty harbour. 'It's a mistake to try to go back. It was different when my grandmother was alive. Now it's all very sad.'

He put on an understanding face, but he was glad she had lost her enthusiasm for the place. He didn't say, 'I told you so,' but he couldn't resist, 'So we're not going there for our honeymoon after all?'

Anna looked down at her hands without seeing them and thought, Suppose the island is haunted? Suppose I did go back and there was no one at all, and the house over Spanish Sands had been in ruins for years? She said, 'I shan't go back again,' and got up and went to her sketching pad on the table by the window. 'I did two sketches for your mother,' she said, and carefully tore out the portraits of Douglas and Robina.

Douglas was standing by her when she finished detaching Robina, smiling because they were both quite flattering. 'She'll love these. Did you do any more sketches?'

'A few. I got an idea for a wall panel.' She could show him the scenes and the galleons, but she could hardly show him all the pictures of Paul. She closed the pad and put it in a drawer of her bureau. 'I'll show you some time,' she said. 'Are we going out to eat? I'm ravenous!'

'Would you mind if we went home? My mother had a meal ready, and she's very anxious to see you home again safe and sound.' It was nice to be welcomed back, and she said yes, of course, she'd like that.

Douglas's parents were in the drawing room that was going to be redecorated although Anna couldn't see a thing wrong with it, not one mark on the watered silk wallpaper. They both welcomed Anna warmly, his father smiling from behind the evening newspaper, and his mother putting her arms around her and hugging her.

Anna produced her small gifts from her handbag, perfume for Mrs Bissell and Robina and a new aftershave for Mr Bissell, and Douglas handed over the two sketches.

The sketches went down best. Both parents were pleased with them and Mrs Bissell immediately decided to have them framed at the Galleries and then hang them in her bedroom. 'This is really a very nice portrait of Robina,' she said, looking proudly at her daughter's pretty face.

Robina was out on a date tonight, but she had left a message for Anna, her love and she would be phoning in the morning. So Anna ate with Douglas and his mother and father, and after dinner they went back into the drawing room and watched television.

Douglas did ask Anna if she would like to go somewhere they could dance, perhaps. It was Saturday night, there was entertainment to be found, but she wasn't really up to dancing yet.

She stretched out her leg. If you looked closely her ankle was still slightly puffy. 'I twisted it on the island,' she explained. 'That was one of the reasons I came back to the mainland. There's nothing to do on St Morag's but walk.'

They were all sympathetic, although she reassured them that it was fine now. 'How did you manage that?' Douglas asked, and she heard herself say:

'It was the easiest thing. The ground's very rough.'

Once she started talking about the seals one thing would lead to another. She didn't want to talk or think about the day she twisted her ankle, and the night that had followed it.

Douglas drove her home again around midnight. Tomorrow was planned. He was going out to a village in the Cotswolds to collect something for the Galleries, and he would be along for Anna about eleven. They would have lunch on the way and make a day of it.

She would have preferred saying goodnight in the car, but he got out and came into the house with her, and up the stairs to her little bedsitter. She turned on the lights as soon as they stepped into the room, then Douglas closed the door and took her in his arms and kissed her.

It was pleasant being kissed by Douglas. There was no madness in it. It didn't set her blood on fire and drive her mindless.

They kissed what seemed to be close and cosy to Anna but must have stirred Douglas temporarily out of his usual discretion, because when they stopped kissing he said, 'I don't want to leave you. I suppose the world wouldn't end if I stayed.'

She supposed it wouldn't, but she didn't want him to stay and she said gently, 'I've travelled a long way today. I'll see you tomorrow.'

'Yes, of course.' He shouldn't have suggested staying the night. He never had before and he could see now how indiscreet it would have been. For one thing, 'My car standing outside all night might not look so good.'

Anna couldn't think of anybody around who would care much, but Douglas was always concerned about the appearance of things. So was Mrs Bissell. If he didn't go home tonight his mother would ask some questions when he did get back.

She turned away to hide a smile. Her handbag was still hanging on her arm by its thin gilt chain, and she took it across to the table by the window, where the camellia stood, and dropped it among some of the clutter she had unpacked but not yet put away.

Then she froze, as her eye caught the glitter of gold. The doubloon was lying on the table, beside her sewing case. She hadn't brought that away with her. She had deliberately left it behind.

If it was here now Paul must have put it here, and she looked jerkily into the corners of the room as though he might be standing silently watching her from the shadows.

CHAPTER SEVEN

DOUGLAS was the only other person in the room and she said, 'Well, goodnight,' so sharply that it sounded as though she was annoyed. She wanted him to go because she needed to think. Of course she wasn't angry with Douglas, but his conscience was troubling him and he made for the door.

'I'll see you tomorrow, then?' he said with what he hoped was a placating smile. 'Please don't be offended, I shouldn't have suggested staying the night.'

'Of course I'm not offended.' Anna managed a smile, ushering him out, and then stood for what seemed ages before she could find the courage to walk back to the table and take another look at the doubloon. Perhaps she hoped it had all been some trick of the light. Her feet dragged, and she didn't look directly at the clutter on the table top until she was right up against the table.

There was the doubloon. Solid and very real. But this time it was less of a bolt from the blue. First sight of it had shocked her as much as a note with Paul's signature might have done. She had been ready to believe he was either in this room or just outside. But now she tried to think calmly and remember clearly.

She had deliberately left the doubloon when she packed her sketch pads the morning she left the island, but Paul could easily have put it into her bag, when she went out of the kitchen, to the toilet and to collect her oilskins, he could have slipped it in into her sewing case, perhaps. That had been at the bottom of her suitcase, she hadn't taken it out in the hotel. She hadn't un-packed it until last night, tossing it on to the table with other things and, with her mind so preoccupied, she hadn't even noticed when the coin fell out.

Of course that was the logical explanation, and she was glad she'd reached it because she still had butter-flies in the stomach. That showed how jumpy she was about anything connected with Paul Peralta, and some day soon she would mention him around.

Not everything about him, but she would say he was there, just someone else on the island, another holiday-maker. No one in particular, she hadn't particularly liked him. But he might phone her up some time and if she'd never mentioned him it would be too late then to start.

She dropped the doubloon into the drawer with the coloured stones and sequins. She might fasten it on to the Spanish Sands wall panel if she ever got around to making it. Surely there would come a time when the tale would mean no more to her than any other myth or legend. But when she got into bed she pulled the sheet over her head as though she might hear her name called in the night and find herself drawn, resisting but help-less, towards a dark man ...

She was finishing breakfast next morning when she heard the phone ringing and Bill shouting up the stairs, 'Anna, call for you!'

She hurried down the two flights to the phone in the hall and it was Robina calling to say hello. 'Had a nice holiday?' Robina asked.

'Thanks, yes.'

'Glad you're back early.' They hadn't expected Anna till tonight. 'I'll be seeing you later today. We're coming along with Douglas, so we can all have lunch together.'

Who were 'we'? Anna wondered. Mrs Bissell? But Robina was giggling, 'I've got a super new boy-friend.'

She was a pretty girl, she had plenty of new boy-friends, and Anna asked, 'Anyone I know?'

'I've only just met him and I'm not sure that I ought to be introducing him around.' Robina giggled again. 'But you'll have Douglas to keep an eye on you, and Paul isn't your type.'

'Paul?' squeaked Anna, and Robina said dreamily:

'He's the most exciting man I've ever met. Just wait till you meet him! We'll be along with Douglas. 'Bye till then.' After Robina had rung off Anna held the phone in her hand, looking at it thoughtfully. Then she slowly replaced it and went back upstairs, taking each step with deliberate care, thinking, thinking.

Paul was a common enough name, and she had explained the doubloon to herself last night. This was a little coincidence. If the name had been Aloysius or Inigo she might have had something to worry about, but Pauls were all over the place.

He was standing by the window in her room, arms folded, the way she remembered. 'Surprised to see me?' he asked.

No, she wasn't surprised at all, but her heart gave a strange leap and she had to sit down before she could ask, 'What are you doing here?'

'Bed and breakfast for a week or two.'

'In this house?' Joan hadn't mentioned him. It was off season, there weren't many tourists, but occasional ones arrived all year long. They hadn't done much talking last night, what with Douglas coming round to fetch her. Today Joan or Bill might have said, 'We've got a lodger for a week or two.'

'I took the boat back,' Paul said chattily, 'and decided I'd had it with St Morag's. You made it sound interesting down here, so I came to see, and I found the Laurels —just how you'd described it—and Joan took me in.'

Anna glared at him. 'She didn't say anything to me. Did you tell her you knew me?'

'No.'

So there was a conspiracy of silence already, and she demanded furiously, 'What's your game?'

'Writing,' he said, as though that was the complete answer. 'It wasn't going too well on the island, so I decided perhaps I needed the stimulus of people around.'

'Like Robina?'

He smiled, and she was scared for Robina. 'I was walking round the Galleries,' he told her. 'I must say your work is splendid. I can't wait to see what you make of Spanish Sands.'

'I've gone off Spanish Sands,' she snapped. 'And we're talking about Robina.'

'That was where I met her—in the Galleries. I recognised her from your sketch and we started talking.'

'About me?' No, because Robina thought she would be introducing Anna to Paul this afternoon.

'I've said nothing to anybody.' He seemed to be shrugging the whole thing off. 'Please yourself what you tell them.'

He was bad trouble whatever she did and she could cheerfully have throttled him. She jumped up and walked blindly round the room for a few seconds before she could trust herself near him.

Then she looked at him with loathing, her voice thick. 'You're not here because you liked what I told you about this town. You followed me. *Why?*'

'I want things to go well for you. I'm not too sure about Douglas.' That took her breath. It was a lie and it was a foul thing to say. 'Maybe I believe in the old legend,' he said. 'You called me up and now I'm your guardian angel,' and she hooted derisively.

'Guardian demon more like!' He was no friend, wanting things well for her. He was an opportunist, wanting something for himself, a user of others. She said fiercely, 'You're blackmailing me. What are you after? Another easy billet? You're not moving in here rent-free.'

'The day I don't pay,' he said, 'I'll move out.'

'Pay with what? What do you use for money?'

'The usual stuff.' He grinned. 'Don't worry, I'm not here to sponge on you nor embarrass you. We can meet for the first time today if you like.'

Anna was in a state of confusion, but she had enough sense to see where that could lead. 'Once I went along with that I would be in trouble. When Robina produces you I shall tell them we've met, and I'll tell them I don't trust you, and you can start explaining why you never said a word about me.'

'All of it?'

It could be told so that it sounded unforgivable, and she felt hollow and sick. She said, 'You make me sick!'

'I'm sorry. You haven't told anybody about me?'

'No.'

'Why didn't you?'

'Because I wanted to come home and forget I ever went back to St Morag's.' She looked at him, agonised, and he said softly :

'But you can't do that, my bonny bird.'

'I could have done. Why——?' She shook her head, shaking away the angry tears that threatened, and Paul said quite gently :

'I'm a rootless man, I've always gypsied around, but I wouldn't harm you, and that's the truth. Tell them as much or as little as you like. It doesn't matter a damn to me.'

She must think what she was going to say before Douglas came, and perhaps Paul would leave the telling to her. He might not want Robina to know that only a few days ago Anna had been barring her bedroom door against him.

Unfortunately that wasn't the whole story. If she told them that he might recall the night she had begged, 'Don't leave me,' and they had lain in one bed till morning. And who would believe sleep was all they had shared?

She asked, 'Where's your room?'

'On the floor below. Number 5.'

'Then stay in it,' she said with gritted teeth, 'and keep out of my room. Why did you come in here and leave the doubloon last night?'

'To warn you I was here.' She hadn't really believed she had brought it with her. She had known he was around.

He was going now, walking towards the door, tossing over his shoulder, 'Tell them what you like. You could have trouble with Douglas, but it wouldn't matter with Robina.'

Then she was alone, her head whirling. It was no use saying she had met Paul in casual holiday fashion on St Morag's because if their relationship had been simple and straightforward he would have mentioned it. By keeping quiet he had ensured that everybody would think there was plenty to hide. And of course there was, but not as much as everyone would believe.

She would have to tell them. About the seals, about getting stuck in his house. But she could say she'd left St Morag's as soon as the fog lifted and the boat could do the crossing, because there were only the two of them on the island and it was an awkward situation.

She hadn't expected to see Paul again, she hadn't invited him here, and then he could start explaining what the hell he thought he was doing.

Making it with Robina, apparently. *Damn* Paul. What *had* brought him down here? Sheer mischief? The unfinished business of getting her into bed when she was neither running a temperature nor a panic? Had he thought it would be a laugh to give her the fright of her life by turning up to get a look at Douglas?

When he spotted Robina in the Galleries perhaps he

couldn't let a bird in the hand slip away. He knew
enough about Robina from what Anna had said to start
with an unfair advantage. Robina was a sitting pigeon,
and very pretty and comfortably off. Her father gave her
a generous allowance and Douglas and his sisters all had
money inherited from grandparents.

Paul could do a lot worse than Robina, but Robina
could hardly do worse than Paul. He was a layabout, and
a womaniser. What about Gemma? If it hadn't been
for finding that letter from Gemma Anna would have
ended up having an affair with him herself.

She felt guilty about that. She didn't want to think
about that, and she couldn't sit here brooding much
longer. She sat at the table by the window for what
seemed a very long time. She was dressed, her make-up
finished except for the final touches of lipstick and
perfume, and now she went to the mirror and coloured
her none-too-steady lips.

She was wearing a tweed suit in mulberry with a soft
full skirt and long lean jacket, and a lilac blouse. It was
a cold day and she might need a mac or a thick scarf
to wrap around her when she got out of the car.

If she got into the car. After the balloon went up it
was very unlikely that the four of them would be off
for a jolly day's outing. More likely there would be a
long cross-questioning from Douglas. Why hadn't she
said anything last night about there only being the two
of them on the island? Why hadn't she said a word
about Paul? Why hadn't Paul mentioned her? Why had
Paul followed her here and immediately taken up with
Robina?

'I don't *know*!' she wailed at her reflection in the
mirror, and a great wave of misery swept over her as
though nothing would ever be right again.

She was probably being stupid. Why shouldn't
Douglas understand?

As soon as he arrived she would tell him all about Paul, and she sat waiting, stitching a cushion cover to occupy herself and making a botched job of it.

If Douglas had come alone she would have started right away, but the three of them came in together. They must have collected Paul on the way up. Anna was aware of Douglas and Robina, but they seemed to be pale smudged figures in the background. Although Douglas came over and kissed her her face swung towards Paul so that Douglas missed her lips and planted his kiss on her cheek.

Paul was wearing a black sweater and beautifully cut slacks, with a three-quarter camel coat slung over his shoulders like a cloak. He looked handsome, devastating, and when their eyes met his gave out a sense of danger that stopped Anna breathing.

Robina said proudly, 'This is Paul Peralta—Paul, I've told you about Anna,' and Paul came across the room to her and she couldn't say a word. Her chance was over within seconds. As soon as she hesitated it was lost, and then Paul said, 'Hello, Anna,' and all she could say was, 'Hello.'

'Paul's a writer,' Robina announced. She was with him now, her hand slipped through his arm, fingering the stuff of his jacket, and Anna had a savage impulse to knock her hand away as Robina chattered on, 'He writes for television.'

'Really?' said Anna. 'What?' She had asked Paul, but Robina answered:

'He's got a play coming on in a few months' time,' and that was a lie because Paul was holding back laughter. Anna could see it, looking at him. He had been spinning a yarn to Robina, he'd got no television play coming up.

'Do they pay well?' she drawled.

'I get by.'

'I'm sure you do,' she said meaningfully, and both Douglas and Robina stared at her, then Douglas said:

'Ready, darling?'

'Nice room,' said Paul, looking around as though this was the first time he had seen it. 'Robina tells me you sew for a living.'

'That's right.' Anna took the scarf that was lying on the sofa and draped it round her shoulders and he picked up the cushion cover she had been embroidering. 'What happened here?' he asked.

'The silk tangled. It does sometimes.' She whipped it from him and he said:

'I know someone who does invisible darning. She uses hairs and she makes a very neat job. You ought to meet her. You'd have something in common.'

'We could compare notes.' Anna smiled rigidly, showing a lot of teeth, and Robina pouted and asked:

'A good friend?'

He grinned. 'About to get married.'

'Well, she'll keep her husband's clothes nicely mended,' said Anna, and Paul sounded shocked.

'He's not the kind of bloke to need a jacket darned. She's doing very well for herself.'

'I'm pleased for her,' said Anna. 'Whoever she is.'

Before the day was over Douglas and Robina were going to realise this wasn't a first-time meeting, and it might be simpler to tell them now instead of doing double-talk with Paul until somebody demanded, 'What goes on with you two?'

But Paul was taking Robina out of the room and Douglas asked, 'Got everything?'

'My handbag.' It was on the table by the window. As she fetched it Douglas said quietly, 'What do you think of him?'

'What do you?' she countered, and Douglas sucked in air before he admitted:

'I don't know, but I should think he could be a tough customer.'

Anna bit the inside of her mouth to hold down the

laughter. This wasn't funny, but there was something hysterically comic in the way Paul was playing it to the edge to see if she would crack. He was a devil, he wanted her to start babbling. It would amuse him and it wouldn't hurt him with Robina.

He could always say Robina had brought him down here. That he had fallen in love with the sketch Anna had made of her and come down determined to meet her. Robina might even believe that. It could be true except that Paul was not the man for sentimental gestures.

'Started locking your door?' Douglas asked approvingly, as she turned the key in the lock and dropped it into her handbag. He'd been on to her before, about leaving her room unlocked, and she'd always said, 'There's nothing much worth stealing.'

'Yes,' she said. She would be locking it from now on. From now on it would be a regular habit.

Paul and Robina were waiting in the hall, talking to Joan who had been carrying a tray out of the dining room. Joan hadn't known till now that her latest lodger was dating Robina Bissell. 'I didn't know you two knew each other,' she'd greeted them, and Paul had smiled and whispered behind his hand, 'It was a pick-up, in the Galleries,' with which Douglas and Anna rounded the top of the stairs and began to walk down the second flight.

Joan thought Paul and Robina made an attractive couple, Robina hanging on to his arm. So did Douglas and Anna, with Douglas's hand under Anna's elbow. 'Good for the Galleries,' she said. 'You'll have met Anna, then?'

'We've just been introduced,' and he watched Anna coming down the stairs. They all moved towards the front door, Douglas giving Joan a 'Good morning' in passing and Anna saying, 'Hello, see you later.'

Paul held the door open so that Robina walked through, and as Anna and Douglas hesitated somehow Douglas was edged ahead and Paul had Anna's arm, above the elbow.

It wasn't a gentle guiding. It was a hard hurting grip, and as the door closed behind them she turned on him. He gave her a brief smile and then car doors were being opened, Robina and Paul were in the back seat and Anna was beside Douglas, gripping the chain on her handbag so that she could feel the links biting into her skin.

Paul might not have realised how strong that hold was, but next time he grabbed her she was going to hit out.

Douglas was going over the route as they pulled away from the kerb. The journey should take about one and a half hours, over the plains and through several Wiltshire villages into the Cotswolds. He mentioned the villages, and the byways by which they could avoid the uglier stretches, and Robina kept saying, 'That's a pretty place. That's such a pretty stretch of road.'

Anna looked at herself in the little mirror on her sunshield, and rubbed away a speck of grime from her cheekbone with her little finger. She could see Paul's reflection, and she asked abruptly, 'How did you come to choose the Laurels?'

Nobody had been talking just then. Even if they had been she might have spoken over their voices, because when she looked straight at Paul the others seemed to fade out. It was as though he generated a force field and unluckily she was on his wavelength. 'I was recommended,' he said.

'Who by?' Now she was challenging him. She turned in her seat and waited to see if he would have the nerve to say, 'You,' but he said, 'The Tourist Board. I'm doing some research down here. They gave me several addresses.' Joan was on the Tourist Board list, that was a lucky shot nobody could disprove. 'I thought the Laurels had a homely sound,' he said. 'Would you recommend it?'

'Of course,' she said shortly. 'What kind of research?'

'I'm setting a crime in a respectable Regency town like this.'

'Fact or fiction?' Douglas and Robina thought she was joking, but she wasn't too sure herself, especially when he said:

'Mostly I stick to fiction. Blackmail in this case. A lover turning up from the past.'

Anna hoped she wasn't colouring. Paul was not her lover, but when he said that she was conscious of the lean hard body beneath the clothes he wore, the sensuous longing that his touch unlocked. She turned back abruptly to face the oncoming road and Robina said, 'You didn't tell me that. What happens?'

'I'm not too sure,' Paul laughed, and Robina joined in, and in the mirror Anna saw his dark eyes on her.

Robina was obviously delighted with herself. Through the mirror Anna could see the looks she was sharing with Paul and she raised the sunshield because they were irritating her. It was a cold very bright day and she wished she had brought dark glasses.

Paul got them both talking, Douglas and Robina. He asked questions: about the Gallery, about the villages they were passing through, about their lives; and Anna thought—he got me talking like this too, he's got a mind like a thieving magpie. She was less enchanted by his charm than they were, and she answered briefly when the talk came round to her, but neither Douglas nor Robina seemed to notice.

They stopped for lunch at a thatched pub and sat under the heavy beams of the dining room considering menus, handwritten and described in loving detail under each item.

The starters were all soups, and they were reading the respective contents of farmhouse and country cream when Paul said, 'It's the day for a good hot curry.'

'Do you like curry?' Robina would have been fascinated by any preference he'd expressed. Curry wasn't on the menu and Anna went on reading about soup, head bent. She knew more or less what was coming next.

'One of my favourite dishes,' Paul sighed nostalgically. 'A friend I knew made the most superb curries. Out of this world.' He chuckled. 'Trouble was you never knew what went into them!'

Anna lifted her eyes from the menu and said sweetly, 'You have a friend who can sew *and* a friend who can cook? I presume this is another lady?'

'You presume wrong,' he retorted cheerfully. 'The curry cook was no lady. Do you like curry?'

It was a game he was playing, but for the life of her she couldn't forgo the exhilaration of seeing if she could get away with the last word. 'I ate one once that took the roof off my mouth,' she said. 'I doubt if I'll ever eat another.'

Paul burst out laughing and Douglas asked, 'When was that?'

Douglas didn't like 'made-up' dishes, she'd never had curry with him, so she could reply, 'A long time ago,' And it was surely true, because St Morag's had been another life altogether.

In the end they all had roast beef and Robina promised Paul a curry very soon. Anna wondered who would make it. The Bissells' housekeeper, probably, Robina was no cook. If it had been for Paul alone she would have welcomed the chance to lend a hand and get it up to scalding pitch.

The object of the journey was to collect a pair of handmade lutes from the workshop. One was ordered and the other was going on display in the Galleries, and the workshop was an old chapel in a road leading from a village green.

The craftsmen were waiting, two brothers with identical balding heads and bushy beards, and the chapel door opened as the car drew up. Until four years ago they had mainly produced guitars, then a growing public interest in musical instruments of a bygone age had persuaded them to specialise in lute-making. Each lute took two to three weeks and they were never going to make a fortune.

But they were proud of their work, and the two lutes lying on the workbench were beautiful. One neck was sycamore, one beech, both with blackwood inlaid fingerboards. 'Ah yes,' said Douglas. The Galleries had been selling the Widcote brothers' lutes almost as long as they had been making them, and these two looked well up to standard.

'You'd better hear them first,' said Maurice Widcote. He sat on the high stool and played a tune none of them knew, but it brought a lump to Anna's throat. On the second he played a livelier air, she could imagine dancing to it, round a maypole on the village green out there.

'Sounds fine,' said Douglas when Maurice put down the lute, and Paul asked, 'What was the music?'

'Early sixteenth century,' said Frank, the other brother. Robina giggled.

'They'll never make the charts!'

'Shall we get them packaged?' said Douglas.

They needed careful wrapping, and while Frank put them in boxes, with padding around, it seemed that Maurice was giving Paul a conducted tour, explaining the process of manufacture from the X-ray photographs of lutes on the walls via the well-worn tools and sharp scalpels.

Paul must have started him off by asking a question,

Paul was still asking questions, his enthusiasm matching that of the dedicated craftsman who was walking around the workroom with him.

He gets everything going out of life, thought Anna. Whether he was turning on arrogant sex appeal, or simply listening and learning, Paul had a magnetism it was impossible to ignore and very hard to resist.

Robina was still literally hanging on to him, and Anna would have enjoyed listening to what Maurice Widcote was telling them, but she wasn't trailing along behind. She walked around the workroom alone, until Douglas and Frank carried out the two boxes to the car.

Wood was a living thing. She stroked the back of an unfinished lute, standing on the workbench, and smiled at the feel of it; and Paul leaned across and touched it too and she could have sworn that electricity ran between their hands. Her own fingers tingled as she took them away.

The sun was setting when they left. Nobody did much talking. The road wound and at times the rays of the sunset came dazzlingly through the window. If Anna had the sunshield down she couldn't avoid seeing the two in the seat behind, with Robina's head on Paul's shoulder, and it annoyed her.

Not that she cared whose head was on Paul's shoulder, but there was going to be trouble there and she was partly responsible. She would have to talk to Douglas and nobody was going to thank her for talking. Not Robina, not Paul, certainly not Douglas.

She snapped up the screen and the mirror, and the setting sun nearly blinded her so that she put her hand in front of her eyes and turned her head.

'What's the matter?' Douglas's voice was sharp with alarm. 'Are you all right?'

He slackened speed, his glance swivelling nervously from Anna to the road, and she said, 'Yes, I'm all right.'

Then it dawned on her that he thought her eyes were bothering her. She said, 'It was the sun. What did you think it was? Very delayed action from my accident?'

'Hush, darling.' He indicated the seat behind with a slight jerk of his head, as though she had brought up an embarrassing subject. That was ironic, considering Paul knew all about it. She turned, with an arm across the back of her seat. Robina's eyes were closed, but the lids were twitching. Paul was wide awake, his dark eyes very steady.

'I was in a car crash a while ago,' said Anna chattily. 'I was driving, not Douglas, so don't worry, it isn't likely to happen again. I had a bang on the head and I could have gone blind, so wasn't I lucky that I can still see as well as ever?'

'Very lucky,' agreed Paul.

'For Godsake!' Douglas exploded. Anna had never seen Douglas so angry before, his hands clenched on the wheel and his cheeks mottled with little patches of red. 'Paul doesn't want to hear about that. You were in an accident and you got away with it, and other people's accidents are about as interesting as other people's dreams.'

'Sorry,' she said.

Paul looked mildly intrigued by this outburst, Robina's eyes stayed shut although her lids were flickering like mad. 'How about some music?' asked Anna, and fiddled with the radio until she found some.

Even less was said after that, and it was Douglas who eventually broke the silence. He began to talk about the lute makers. 'Interesting couple, the Widcotes, aren't they?'

'Fascinating,' Anna murmured when nobody answered from the back seat, and Douglas went on about this upsurge in the demand for craftsmen-made instruments in recent years.

'It's back to the grass roots,' he explained. 'The public's fed up with mass production. Something beautifully made by hand is a sure sale. Like your sewing, darling.'

'Thanks,' she said. She could have been alone with Douglas in this car. Robina was almost certainly asleep in Paul's arms and it was considerate of Paul to stay quiet and not disturb her. She didn't think that Paul was asleep, he wasn't the dozing kind, and her fingers itched to turn the radio to full blast so that Robina would wake and jump up and for the moment at least jerk away from Paul.

She didn't analyse that impulse. She was irritated, that was all. Probably with Douglas for having snapped at her when she'd mentioned her accident. She said, 'It's nice to know my work's a sure sale. So long as my hands and eyes last.'

Douglas sighed and she relented. He was obviously sorry he'd lost his temper, and she was sorry she hadn't been more understanding, because of course her car crash wasn't a happy subject. She had nearly died and Douglas had been very distressed, and there was no sense harking back to it. It should be forgotten.

She rested her head on Douglas's shoulder and said, 'It's nice to be home again.'

'It's nice having you back,' said Douglas, and from the back seat Paul said, 'You must tell us about your holiday some time.'

'Why, hello,' said Anna, 'I'd forgotten you were there.'

They went to the Bissells' home and Anna wondered how often Paul had been here. He could only have met Robina a few days ago, but he walked in as though he knew the place well. 'We'll go into the study, shall we?' said Douglas.

Paul knew where the study was. They were in the hall and he turned towards the right door, and Mrs Bissell came out of the drawing room and said, 'I heard the car. Hello, Anna dear.'

Anna went obediently for a kiss on the cheek. 'Hello, Paul,' said Mrs Bissell, and Anna thought she looked uneasily at him. If she did her mother instinct was right.

Nobody ever did any studying in the study, it got its name because there was an antique desk in there and glass-fronted bookselves. There were also comfortable armchairs, and a music centre disguised as another piece of antique furniture. A fire was burning in the Adam fireplace.

Anna sat down and Robina pulled Paul down beside her into the two-seater settee opposite.

'Scotch all right for everybody?' asked Douglas.

The men had whisky with a little water, the girls with a lot of ginger ale, although Anna felt she could have done with hers straight tonight. She couldn't relax, sitting here wondering what Paul was going to say. As it happened he said nothing with a double meaning, but the sight of him, his arm along the back of the settee behind Robina, with Robina nestled up against him, kept her in a state of prickling agitation.

The housekeeper brought in a tray of sandwiches and they played tapes and records while they ate, and sipped their drinks. When Douglas put on, 'One of Anna's favourites, Songs of the Isles,' she couldn't look at Paul. It was only background music, Robina and Douglas talked all through it, but she was thankful when it ended.

They were talking about the Galleries. Starting with the Widecote brothers they went on to other artists and craftsmen who sold through Bissells. Most were interesting, some eccentric. There were any number of stories to be told, and Paul listened, as he always did, as though he found every anecdote enthralling.

He commented, 'It sounds a pretty exclusive club,' and Douglas beamed, gratified.

'We are exclusive. We only handle the very best.'

'Like Anna,' said Paul, smiling at her, and Douglas beamed even wider.

'She's going to be an international name before she's through. She's a very talented girl, is my Anna.'

Anna was twisting her ring. Douglas saying, 'my Anna', as though he owned her made her want to say, 'No!' loud and clear.

'Oh, Anna's exceptionally clever,' said Robina, and it sounded more like a sneer than a compliment. 'We can sell everything Anna makes. She's the girl with the golden needle.' She giggled, draining her drink, and Anna remembered that Robina usually got the giggles after a drink, although this one had seemed innocuous. She herself was stone cold sober, and she wondered if Robina was being particularly silly and giggly because she imagined Paul liked silly little women.

You're wrong there, thought Anna. Paul doesn't need dim folk around to make him feel bright. He wouldn't begrudge a woman talent.

'Anna can draw portraits as well,' said Robina. 'She did one of me while she was on holiday. Mother's getting it framed. Would you like to see it?' She fluttered her eyelashes at Paul and he said:

'Yes.'

Robina only brought her own picture back, not Douglas's. 'Like it?' she asked, handing it over to Paul.

'It's a good likeness.'

'Do you really think so?' Robina sat down beside him, her face raised to his, pouting, 'I'm not sure about the mouth. I think she's made me look too thin-lipped.'

No, I haven't, thought Anna. You are thin-lipped. I've followed the lipstick line which makes your mouth prettier than it is. What was Robina trying to do, her lips provocatively parted so close to Paul's? Get him to kiss her, of course, and of course he would, and Anna

said, 'Would you recognise her from my sketch?' so
that Paul turned his head and sat back a little and said:

'No doubt at all.'

'I thought you might.' Neither Douglas nor Robina
could get the inner meaning of that, but Anna's voice
had an edge that made the silence that followed uncomfortable until Douglas said:

'You did some other sketches while you were away,
didn't you? Didn't you tell me you had an idea for a
wall panel?'

'Spanish Sands,' said Anna, and went on looking at
Paul. 'Where a galleon from the Armada sank off St
Morag's.'

Douglas chuckled. Usually Anna was the last girl to
cause awkward silences or make barbed remarks. She
got on easily with everybody, but something was riling
her tonight, and he supposed it was because he had lost
his temper with her when she'd mentioned that her sight
had been in danger.

He tried to lighten the atmosphere with a chuckle and
the quip, 'Half the Armada must have been blown up
to Scotland if every island that claims a galleon actually
has one.'

'St Morag's has,' said Anna. 'There was wreckage
brought up in fishing nets not all that long ago. My
grandmother told me about a barnacle-covered piece of
wood with "Santa" carved on the side.'

'I've heard of the dark men,' said Paul.

'Who?' asked Robina.

Anna sat with her hands clasped round her knees. She
and Paul looked fixedly at each other, although Robina
was still cuddling up to Paul and Douglas was leaning
towards Anna. 'The dark men who sailed in the galleon,'
she said. 'They call during the storms and if a girl
answers she's haunted for ever.'

'It sounds thrilling,' Robina gurgled. 'Do they leave
seaweed on her pillow?'

'Or doubloons,' said Paul, and the dark eyes were suddenly too much for Anna. You could be haunted by a living man as easily as by a ghost, if the imprint went deep enough. She wanted him to go away, to leave here, to stop troubling her. But she couldn't imagine ever being able to forget him. Even if her mind blocked him out her body could still go on hungering, and that scared and shocked her. She got up and said, 'It's been a lovely day, but I think I'd better get home now.'

As Paul was staying where she lived Paul might have walked back with her. But he showed no intention of leaving Robina yet, so Douglas said, 'All right.'

Anna said goodnight to Paul and Robina and as they walked out to the car Douglas said, 'I hope Robina knows what she's doing with that fellow.'

'You must be joking,' muttered Anna. 'She might not know him too well, but she certainly knows what she's doing with him.'

Douglas sighed. Anna was *not* herself tonight. She sat silent in her seat and he supposed she was still sulking. As the car passed the slightly tilting lamp-post against which her car had smashed he said, 'I'm sorry I spoke the way I did when you mentioned your accident.'

'Forget it,' she said. 'I thought you over-reacted, but that's not to say you weren't right. Other people's accidents aren't very interesting.' What had started her babbling away about her smash-up was Douglas twitching with alarm when she'd put her hand in front of her eyes. She was still sensitive about her eyes, that she might have lost her sight, that she might have lost Douglas too.

He said, 'I still can't bear to talk about it. God, what I went through!'

Me too, she thought. She said, 'I won't bring it up again, we'll pretend it never happened,' and while Douglas smiled he wondered if she was being ironic.

She left him in the car, reflecting wryly as she climbed

the stairs to her room that if he got into such a state just thinking about her losing her sight he wouldn't have been much support if it had actually happened.

Tomorrow she was starting work in earnest. There were still some outstanding orders from the exhibition which had to be dealt with, and another thing she hadn't managed to finish before she went on her convalescing holiday to St Morag's was Robina's blouse. After that there was her wedding dress, she supposed.

She brought out the blouse and sat stitching a minute cross-stitch geometric pattern on the sleeve edging and in a panel down the front. She thought about Robina a lot as she worked, because she couldn't believe that Paul was serious about Douglas's sister.

He hadn't seemed serious. For some reason of his own he was stringing Robina along, and Anna wanted to know if he proposed treating her as he had Gemma, another walk-out. Robina thought he was a wonderful man, understanding her like nobody had before, but that was because Anna had told him so much about her.

Anna had to talk to him about Robina, and when she did she would hand him that doubloon back. She didn't want it. What he had said tonight about the dark ghosts leaving doubloons gave her the shivers.

She should be talking to him tonight because tomorrow she was going to tell Douglas about St Morag's and it was only fair to warn Paul. If he *was* serious about Robina it would give him a chance to get his story straight.

She finished the blouse just after midnight, and wrapped it up carefully. Then she took the doubloon out of the 'glitter' drawer and went downstairs with it. A small light burned on each landing, but the house was very quiet as she tapped lightly on door number five. No one answered, and after a little while she tried again a little louder.

Paul might be sleeping, but it was likelier that he wasn't back, that he was still with Robina. He could be with Robina for hours yet and then walk back through the silent echoing streets.

Suddenly Anna knew that the room was empty. She had raised her hand to rap on the door again, but she didn't because she knew, as clearly as though she could see him with Robina, in the study in Robina's home, the fire fallen into embers and the lights dimmed. They would be alone. Robina might be the baby of the family, but she was twenty-two. Nobody was going to sit up protecting Robina from a man with whom she wanted to make love.

Anna was shaking. She was cold. And she was angry, because Paul had landed her in a peck of trouble. She didn't know how she was going to start explaining to Douglas, and there need not have been any trouble at all if Paul had told everybody right from the beginning that he had met Anna on St Morag's. There was no reason why they shouldn't have met; by hushing it up he had made everything secretive and suspicious.

Her fingers brushed the doubloon in her jacket pocket and she went to the window on the turn of the stairs, pushing back the stiff latch and raising the heavy lower frame a few inches. Just enough to get her hand through and toss out the doubloon into the overgrown garden below. She didn't want it. She had come down here to get rid of it. If Paul wasn't around to take it then she didn't care where it went so long as it was out of her hands. Throwing it away was a childish gesture, but she thought she felt better for it.

Even so she needed to take a sleeping pill, to stop herself lying awake thinking about Paul and Robina, and listening for his footsteps coming down the street.

CHAPTER EIGHT

NEXT morning Anna decided to take the embroidered blouse round to Robina. Now it was finished there was no reason for leaving it lying about, and Robina might wear it for some of the earlier Christmas parties.

Besides, Anna wanted to talk to her about this affair with Paul. Paul wasn't likely to be staying more than a few weeks, and Robina's attachments were usually brief, so perhaps there was no cause for concern. All the same Anna would be happier if Robina would tell her that.

Paul's door was closed when she passed it. She presumed he was back now. Mrs Bissell wouldn't approve of him staying for breakfast. He was probably having breakfast downstairs, but Anna didn't want to meet him and she hurried out of the house, pulling her coat collar up when she stepped into the cold street where small snowflakes were drifting slowly down.

She called in at Zoe's shop on her way to the Bissells'. The single window had a candle shape of bright red glitter in one corner with silver glitter like smoke and proclaiming 'Happy Christmas'. Candles, all colours and sizes, and assorted candlesticks, were their main line, but it was also a second-hand bookshop, with shelves of books and boxes of 'Mixed Mags'.

When Anna walked in Pete was in the shop and Zoe was in the little office behind, on her knees, sorting and pricing a box of old books. She looked up with a smile. 'Hello, have a good holiday?'

'You'd never believe the half of it,' said Anna fervently.

Zoe's gamine face, under the ragged hairstyle, lit up. 'Try me!'

'Right,' said Anna. 'I'll try it out on you before I tell it to Douglas.' She sat down at the desk. 'First off,' she said, 'when I reached St Morag's it was shut for the winter. Shut down. The houses that aren't falling apart are summer lettings these days, like my cottage.'

There was a flask on the desk, and Zoe was pouring coffee into two mugs. She put one in front of Anna. 'Thanks,' said Anna. 'So there were only the two of us on the island. This man and me.' As she went to pick up the mug Zoe shrieked:

'So what was he like?' Anna's expression answered that and Zoe gasped, 'Go on.' She put her own hand on the coffee mug. This was fascinating. She wasn't having Anna breaking off to drink coffee at this stage.

'I fell in the sea,' said Anna, 'and caught a chill, and I turned my ankle and there was thick fog, it wasn't safe to move around, so I moved into Paul's house and he sort of nursed me.' She hesitated and Zoe looked as though she wanted to shake her.

'Go on!' hissed Zoe.

'Then when the fog lifted he got me over to Carra and I got the plane to Glasgow and stayed there until Saturday.'

'What does sort-of-nursed-you mean?' Zoe felt that the action in this story was all on the island. She wasn't interested in what happened when the fog lifted.

'Tied up my ankle,' said Anna. 'Fed me. Looked after me.'

'Did you sleep with him?' Zoe asked bluntly, and Anna felt her face flame. This was going to happen every time she was asked that, or even when she realised that was what somebody was wondering. What was the use of saying, 'Yes, soundly, from the moment he got into my bed until he got out of it.' Nobody was going to believe her when her cheeks were a fiery guilty scarlet.

Zoe let her take the mug of coffee and Anna got down a couple of gulps. Then Anna said, 'That isn't the problem. The problem is I arrive back here and he's been here ever since I left the island. He walked into the Galleries and walked off with Robina. They're thick as thieves now, and he hasn't told anybody he knows me —*and* he's staying at the Laurels—and neither have I told anyone so far. Except you.'

Zoe's eyebrows were rising until they were lost in her jagged fringe. She said, very slowly, 'Because Douglas wouldn't like it?'

'He would not,' Anna agreed.

'Did what's-his-name—Paul—come down here after you?'

'Maybe.' He wouldn't be here if he hadn't met Anna, but she suspected his motives. She said, 'I talked to him about my friends. He's got this knack of getting people to talk. I told him a lot about Robina. And the Bissells are pretty well off and she's got money of her own. He was living up there rent-free. He says he's always gypsied around, but I shouldn't think he's just what the Bissells ordered for Robina.'

Zoe shrugged, 'She's old enough to look out for herself. Does he do anything for a living?'

'He writes, he says.' Anna had no proof of that, she'd never seen anything he'd written, but he did scribble in notebooks and he did keep cuttings. 'He says he's been all manner of things, a barman, a labourer, an actor.'

'An actor?' Zoe echoed, frowning, then her face cleared, 'That could be it.'

'That could be what?'

'I think I've seen him with her. They stopped to look into the shop window and I thought I'd seen him before somewhere. Has he done anything on T.V.?'

'I don't know.' When Paul first smiled Anna too had

had a nagging feeling that she ought to recognise him. Perhaps he affected all women like that. 'I don't know what he's done,' she said wearily. 'The question is what am I going to do about him?'

'How do you feel about him?' Zoe's eyes were bright. 'It was just a holiday thing, I suppose? You're not thinking of splitting with Douglas?'

It wasn't 'just' anything. It was turning Anna's world upside down. But she said, 'Of course I'm not breaking with Douglas.'

'Then the sooner you tell him you met Paul while you were away the better,' Zoe advised briskly. 'The way it is you're making it look as though you've got a lot to hide, and you're playing into this fellow's hands if he should turn nasty.'

Anna knew she had to tell Douglas. She had just been putting it off. 'Yes,' she said.

'What's his name?' asked Zoe.

'Paul Peralta.'

Zoe's forehead wrinkled and she shook her head. 'Don't think I've ever heard of him.'

'Lucky you,' said Anna.

She was meeting Douglas for lunch. She'd tell him then. When she left Zoe's she carried on with her original intention of taking the blouse along to Robina and having a chat with her. Robina worked part-time at the Galleries, but at a quarter past nine she would still be at home. On the days she did come in she never started work before ten, and this morning when Anna asked for her she was shown into the breakfast room, where Robina sat alone at the table, still wearing a blue silk nightdress and negligee.

She had toast in a toast rack but nothing on her plate, and she was sipping a glass of grapefruit juice as though it tasted sour. When Anna walked in Robina's expression didn't change.

'I've brought your blouse,' said Anna.

'What blouse?'

'The one I was embroidering for you.'

'Oh, that.' Robina looked with complete lack of interest at the bag containing the blouse, that Anna had just put on the table. 'I'd forgotten that.'

Anna smiled. 'Just as well, seeing how long it took me to finish it.'

Robina yawned. 'Excuse me, I had a late night.'

'I can believe that,' said Anna.

'I don't care much whether you believe it or not,' said Robina, and gave her a disdainful stare, as though she was sub-standard merchandise; and Anna knew there was going to be no easy way of explaining why Paul Peralta should not be trusted.

'About Paul——' she began, and Robina snapped:

'I don't really want to hear what you think about Paul either. And neither does he.'

So they had talked about Anna, and that meant St Morag's, and Anna said, 'Oh dear,' and thought how inadequate that was. She should be trying to explain how she had been manoeuvred into this indefensible position, but she was tongue-tied.

'You're jealous, aren't you?' Robina taunted. 'You may be clever Anna but you're not that clever. You're lucky you've still got Douglas, and don't think you can't lose him because you nearly did, so you had better leave Paul alone.'

After this she was certainly going to lose Douglas, and Robina would never like or trust her again. She would probably never come to this house again, but she couldn't get out of it quickly enough now. She had to get back to her own home and calm herself down before she could face Douglas at lunchtime.

In the hall of the Laurels the dining room door was open. A man and woman were finishing breakfast at a table by the window, and Paul sat with a newspaper at another table. They all looked at her as she walked in. Paul smiled, until she reached him and said, 'You've really screwed things up for me, haven't you?'

'Have I?' He sounded more amused than surprised, and she was so angry she wouldn't have cared if the room had been full.

'You told them about St Morag's. You said you'd leave it to me, but you told them.'

'No,' he said, and then she was the surprised one, stammering :

'Well, Robina knows. She's just told me to keep my clever claws off you, and that I'm lucky to still have Douglas and don't think I can't lose him.'

'Now isn't that interesting?' said Paul softly. 'Shall we go up to your room? This needs discussing and your room's warmer than mine.'

He didn't feel the cold. He let wet clothes dry on him, but Anna shrugged as she turned away, and he followed her; and the couple at the table by the window, both holding forks frozen just short of their lips, watched them go.

Anna opened her door and took off her coat, shaking the snowflakes from her shoulders, then putting it on a hanger and hooking it over the wardrobe door. She knew that Paul was waiting for her to speak, and she burst out, 'Then what *has* got into Robina? She's just accused me of being jealous. About you.'

'That's nonsense,' said Paul equably, 'when you're so crazy about Douglas.'

'Of course it's nonsense!' She wasn't crazy about Douglas, she wasn't sure what she was about Douglas. Her voice rose and cracked, 'Why did you *come* here? What do you want with Robina? Are you in *love* with her?'

He said, 'No,' and she said :

'That was the wrong word anyway. Of course you're not. Of course you fancy her or she wouldn't have been so bleary-eyed this morning, but you'd probably fancy any pretty girl, so why Robina? Are you a fortune-hunter?'

Paul burst out laughing. 'A fortune-hunter? That's a nice old-fashioned description. Rather like "mistress". Oh mistress mine.'

'Stop laughing!' she snapped furiously. 'Do you stir things up just for the hell of it? Is that why you picked on Douglas's sister?'

He stopped laughing, and he sounded serious. 'Whether you believe me or not I came down here because I was worried about you.' She gestured exasperation and disbelief, but he went on, 'I tell you I do. It's that flaming legend. It started the night you insisted on walking back home. I thought you were a fool and it would serve you right if you fell off a cliff, but I still followed to make sure you didn't.'

'You *didn't*!' She had looked round and she hadn't seen him. But she thought the ghosts were following her, so perhaps she had heard footsteps.

'I thought you'd turn back,' he explained. 'I never expected you to stagger the whole way.' He grinned, 'Well, you didn't stagger, did you? You ran. And sang.' He whistled a few bars of the tune with which she had tried to keep up her spirits, and she began to smile. 'Then when you got inside I had to walk all the way back to Spanish Sands. I thought then—you want to watch this, mate, this girl is going to be a damned nuisance.'

He had followed her to the cottage that dark night, and she said, slowly, 'You really did come down here to make sure I was all right?'

'Yes, I did.' There was a bond between them; Anna had felt it all along. 'I'm your dark demon,' he said, and they both laughed and she thought, I wish I hadn't thrown the doubloon away, I hope I can find it. She said,

'Why did you think things might not go well for me after I left St Morag's?'

Because she had told him about hearing Douglas say it would have been a hellish life with a blind wife? She had never meant to tell anyone that, but she had told him, and he asked now, 'Are your eyes still worrying you?'

'*No!*' Paul stood still, with folded arms, and she began to fiddle with things, picking up and putting down, moving around the room. 'It's just that sometimes I start thinking how awful it could have been.'

'And you don't believe Douglas would have faced it with you?'

'Of course he would!' There was passionate assurance in her voice, but not in her heart. She was at the table by the window, examining the camellia for freshly opening buds.

'Will you listen to a theory?' asked Paul quietly.

'I don't think I want to.' But he went on:

'I believe he'd have jilted you if you'd gone blind, and subconsciously you want to put him to the test.'

'Rubbish!'

'Shall I tell you what Robina told me before you came back?'

'About me?' Anna sniffed at the largest blossom although she knew it had no scent.

'About the girl who's engaged to her brother, and the car crash and afterwards.'

Terror got her by the throat. She turned towards him then, white-faced. 'My eyes are all right? She didn't tell you they aren't all right?'

He looked at her steadily. 'Yes, they are,' he said, and Anna believed him, which was crazy really, getting more reassurance from him than she had from the doctors. 'So everything's fine,' he said, 'and Douglas will be marrying you at Easter.'

But if she had been blind there would have been no

marriage. 'Don't think you can't lose Douglas, you nearly did,' Robina had just said, and it was after the accident that Anna had nearly lost him. The family knew that.

So did Paul, standing there, pitying her, and her pride rose and she wanted to deny it still, because he had no right to be stripping her of pride. She said, 'Thanks, friend,' and swallowed and smiled. 'You won't be around for the wedding, I suppose?'

'Is there going to be a wedding?'

'Just as soon as I've finished sewing my wedding dress.' She crossed to the cupboard and took out the cardboard box. 'Would you like to see it?' She lifted the seedpearl bodice and he said:

'You've got a lot more to do.'

'So I'd better get on with it.'

'Yes,' he said. He went, and she moved like an automaton, carrying the box to the window, threading the needle, opening the little box of pearls. She worked for five minutes or so, her fingers doing it all, her mind knowing that she would never wear this dress, that she could hardly bear to look at it.

Before she went on holiday her eyes had blurred while she was sewing her wedding dress. Paul was right. It was subconscious. All in the mind. Deep down she had known that Douglas would have failed her when her need was greatest and because of that she couldn't marry him. She didn't want to marry him. She put the seedpearl bodice back between its folds of tissue paper, and closed the cupboard door on it.

This was the simple answer she had been looking for when she fled to St Morag's. This was what her grandmother would have told her—'You don't want to marry him'. But telling Douglas was going to be tough, and when lunchtime came round Anna had some pretty appliqué work to show for the last two hours but no clear idea what she was going to say to Douglas.

It would probably be better to say it in his office than in a crowded restaurant, and he was alone, checking and signing letters. He gave her a vague smile as she walked in and said, 'Be with you in a minute.'

She waited for him to put his signature on the letter he was reading, then she put the engagement ring down on the desk beside him. 'What's this?' he asked.

'I'm giving it back to you.'

'Why?' He didn't sound all that surprised, and she said :

'You said the accident changed me. It did. I thought we could take up again, the way things were before, but we can't.'

He seemed to know that. He had nodded heavily as she spoke, and his voice was heavy. 'You can't forget what you heard me say that night, can you?'

The night she discovered she might have gone blind. She hadn't heard Douglas say much, but he believed she had. 'I would have stood by you,' he said.

No, you would not, Anna thought. Not for ever. Not for long. There was a tap on the door and before he called, 'Come in,' Douglas hastily swept the ring into the top drawer of his desk. Anna's lips twitched; Douglas really was bothered about appearances. She went out of the room as the secretary brought in a man she didn't know, and Douglas called after her, 'I'll see you later, darling.'

It was like a weight falling off her. She would never have believed one small ring could weigh so much. She went along the road with a light swinging stride. In the grocers they said her holiday had done her a power of good, and the butcher said the cold weather seemed to suit her. She had a smile for them all, she knew that some of her happiness at least was because Paul Peralta had turned out to be her very good friend.

He had come down here because he was worried about her, watching out for her. He was just a friend as yet, but she knew him better than Robina, even if he was spending late nights with Robina. And last night hadn't left Robina in a mellow mood. It had left her waspish and resentful of Anna.

Anna shopped with an eye to tonight's meal. She was asking Paul to dinner, and over dinner she would say, 'You were right about Douglas. He said he'd be seeing me later, but I don't think he'll be asking me to marry him again. And Robina's gone off me too. I hope the Galleries won't stop selling my work.'

There was no danger of that. She sold too well, there were too many markets open to her. She had no worries for the future, but she had plans, and somehow they all seemed to include Paul ...

Zoe came out of Joan's sitting room as Anna walked into the hall of the Laurels. 'I've been waiting for you,' she said. 'Joan and I have been having a good old gossip.' She grinned cheerfully at Joan. 'Come on, then,' she said to Anna. 'I've brought your Christmas prezzie.'

At the top of the first flight of stairs Anna asked, 'What were you gossiping about?'

'Not you,' said Joan. 'Just nattering. I couldn't get in your room. How long have you been locking it?'

'The last day or two.' Anna opened the door and they both went in. 'I haven't got your Christmas present yet.'

'I haven't got yours,' said Zoe, 'unless you'd like to choose a candle.' She had an air of suppressed excitement and Anna felt a slight shiver of foreboding.

'What's the matter?' she asked.

'Now I could be wrong about this,' said Zoe, 'but I was sure I'd seen him before and then you saying he was an actor and a writer, I thought—ah, I know, it was an article.' She was talking about Paul, and Anna put down her shopping and put her gloved hands deep into her pockets.

Zoe was gesticulating, as though she was snatching

ideas out of the air. 'I saw an articule in a magazine, that's where I saw him. So I flipped through all the old magazines. I couldn't find it, so I guess we sold it, but I'm sure I'm remembering it right. Because I can see the photograph, you know. And I think he's Paul Mathieson. It was an article on that T.V. series, the police one—you know it.' She hummed the beginning of the signature tune, and Anna stammered :

'But he's hard-up, that was why he was living on the island.'

Paul Mathieson was a top-liner in the ratings and the earnings, a brilliant tough realistic writer. Zoe said drily, 'The bloke staying here isn't broke, Joan says he runs a Rolls Corniche. It's parked behind the College Arms.'

That was where the Laurels' paying guests usually parked. Nobody had told Anna that Paul had brought a Rolls with him, but she could believe it. With his drive and energy, and razor mind, it was easier to see him as a go-getter than a drifter.

Zoe said, 'I wonder if you'll be in his next book or play or whatever it is,' and Anna remembered the notebooks and thought, so *that*'s why he came, to see how the story ended. All the world's a stage, and he does stir things for the hell of it. It sounded more likely than that rubbish about being worried about her.

'What do you think?' asked Zoe. 'Do you think he is?'

'Let's ask him,' said Anna. 'If he's in.'

He wasn't, and after she had knocked twice on the door Anna opened it. 'Hello!' she called, although she could see at a glance that the room was empty. 'While we're here,' she said, 'we'll make sure.'

Zoe followed her in. 'Shut the door,' said Anna. She took off her gloves and opened the suitcase and Zoe yelped, 'You can't do that!'

'It gets easier,' said Anna. Last time papers were in a

drawer and notebooks. This time she found a notebook on the bottom shelf of a bedside table, beside a mini-recorder. She sat down on the bed to open the notebook and swore softly, 'Hell, it's all in shorthand.'

'Look, I don't think we should——' Zoe broke off to point out, 'You're not wearing your ring.'

'No, I'm not,' Anna agreed. She flipped over the pages but she couldn't decipher a thing, and she stretched out a hand for the mini-recorder, when the door opened and there was Paul, tall, dark and glinting-eyed, enquiring quite pleasantly:

'Looking for something, ladies?'

Zoe fairly hopped back, but Anna sat where she was. 'Mr Mathieson?' she drawled.

'That's right.'

'Peralta!' She gave a short bark of laughter. 'Ha! How could I believe in a name like that?'

'Don't knock it,' he said. 'It was my grandmother's. It seemed a pity to spoil the story. The dark men have to be Spanish and I can claim some Spanish blood.'

Anna smiled with acid sweetness. 'And it's probably more convenient than giving girls your real name. Robina thinks you're Paul Peralta, doesn't she? How about Gemma?'

He smiled too, enquiring gently, 'Do you usually go around reading other people's letters?'

'Not often,' she said, without shame. 'But before I got myself too involved with you I thought I'd like to know a bit more about you, so I did a quick snoop. And look who's talking!' She pounced on the notebook she had dropped on the bed. 'Don't tell me this isn't full of other people's business.' She opened it and glared at the short-hand ciphers, and closed it with a bang and snapped, 'Don't you use anything about me, or anything I told you, or I'll sue you so that you're riding a bicycle instead of swanning around in a Rolls!'

'Look, lady,' Paul stood over her, his voice soft, and to Zoe quite terrifying, 'if I lifted characters from life I'd have been sued for my eye teeth before now.'

'Excuse me,' gulped Zoe. She was near the door and she went through it, and neither Paul nor Anna noticed her go.

'You came down here to be in at the death, didn't you?' Anna gripped her hands together to stop them shaking. 'Douglas and me.'

'Sure,' said Paul promptly. 'And that's why I went out of my way to meet Robina. To get the background.'

'Poor Robina!' Anna felt sorry for Robina.

'Why?' asked Paul. 'I've wined and dined her, and asked for nothing back except that she went on chattering.'

Poor Robina, because she had been willing to give rather more than information. Anna demanded shrilly. 'Then why *are* you here? Just curiosity? Just having to know what happens next? And don't tell me it's because you're my friend for life.'

'All right, I won't.' His voice was very quiet, and his eyes had never been darker. He went on, 'But I thought it was until Douglas walked across the room yesterday and kissed you and I wanted to push his face in. I came here to make sure that Douglas was all right for you, and as soon as he got near you I didn't care if he was the greatest bloke breathing, I knew that if he didn't keep his hands off you sooner or later I was going to half kill him.'

Jealous . . . Paul was jealous . . . Anna couldn't believe it. She stared at him and he said, 'You're not wearing your ring.'

She had to moisten her lips before she could say, 'I gave it back.'

'A good move.' He touched her clenched hands and they fell apart, and he sat down beside her, holding one hand between both his. 'I love you, Anna,' he said.

He was smiling, after a fashion, but she believed him because of the way he said her name. 'From the moment you charged at the seal hunters. A girl that crazy had got to be for me. I couldn't work on St Morag's without you, although I'd gone there to be on my own, to work, away from everybody. There've been a lot of Gemmas in my life, but never anybody I couldn't do without before.'

He was speaking jerkily, not looking into her face, looking at her hand as he held it. 'I can't do without you,' he said. 'You'll never be free of me.'

But of course, the bond between them that had drawn and held her was love. Anna had left St Morag's, but she would have gone back, looking for him, because she loved him in every living cell to the innermost core of her spirit.

She touched his face and he raised eyes so desperate that they broke her heart. Then she touched his lips with her own and words weren't needed.

'Will you marry me?' he asked after a few moments, his mouth still on hers, and she nodded. 'Right away? Then we'll go back to the island for Christmas.' She nodded again. 'I'll get you a ring tomorrow,' he said.

Anna sighed with utter happiness. 'Could you get me another doubloon?' She wrinkled her nose, confessing, 'You aren't the only one who was jealous. I thought you were making love to Robina and I threw it into the garden.'

He whistled and she jerked upright. 'It was only an inexpensive copy? I mean, it wasn't the real thing, not gold, not a genuine old Spanish doubloon?' Her voice was rising in panic.

'It was genuine,' he said, and he was laughing, but this was dreadful. 'It wasn't from the St Morag galleon, but I bought it because it was the next best thing.'

'And you gave it to me and I threw it into the weeds!'

Anna was aghast, horrified. She jumped to her feet. 'Come on, let's go and look for it. It's snowing, we mustn't waste any time.'

Paul got up too, but he stepped in front of her and locked the door, and then he held out his arms to her. 'Later, love,' he said. 'There's something that matters much more.'

He was right. Nothing outside this room compared with what was here, between the two of them. Whatever she needed of comfort and love she would find wherever he was, and she went back into his arms. She would never be free of him so long as she lived, but with him she was free and soaring like a bird.

NEW FROM HARLEQUIN

YOUR 1980 ROMANCE HOROSCOPE!

Harlequin Reader Service

In U.S.A.
M.P.O. Box 707
Niagara Falls, NY 14302

In Canada
649 Ontario Street
Stratford, Ontario, N5A 6W2

Please send me the following Harlequin Romance Horoscope volumes. I am enclosing a check or money order of $1.75 for each volume ordered, plus 40¢ to cover postage and handling.

☐ Aries
(Mar. 21-Apr. 20)
☐ Taurus
(Apr. 21-May 22)
☐ Gemini
(May 23-June 21)
☐ Cancer
(June 22-July 22)

☐ Leo
(July 23-Aug. 22)
☐ Virgo
(Aug. 23-Sept. 22)
☐ Libra
(Sept. 23-Oct. 22)
☐ Scorpio
(Oct. 23-Nov. 21)

☐ Sagittarius
(Nov. 22-Dec. 22)
☐ Capricorn
(Dec. 23-Jan. 20)
☐ Aquarius
(Jan. 21-Feb. 19)
☐ Pisces
(Feb. 20-Mar. 20)

Number of volumes checked @ $1.75 each $_____

N.Y. and N.J. residents add appropriate sales tax $_____

Postage and handling $____.40

TOTAL: $_____

I am enclosing a grand total of $_____

NAME_____

ADDRESS_____

STATE/PROV._____ ZIP/POSTAL CODE_____

ROM 2293